THE BRIDE O
and otl

MONTAGUE SUMMERS (1880-1948) was an English clergyman, occultist, poet and man of letters. His most famous products were a serious of colourful studies of vampirism, lycanthropy and witchcraft, such as *The History of Witchcraft and Demonology* (1926) and *The Vampire: His Kith and Kin* (1928), as well as several volumes of supernatural stories which he edited. He compiled the critical editions of a number of writers, including *Aphra Behn* and *William Congreve*. Alongside these interests, he was also a champion of the English Gothic novel with, amongst other relevant productions, *The Gothic Quest: a History of the Gothic Novel* (1938) and *A Gothic Bibliography* (1941).

DANIEL CORRICK is an editor, philosopher and writer. From 2010 to 2014 he ran Hieroglyphic Press and edited the journal *Sacrum Regnum*. He has published essays on various nineteenth-century figures including Hugo von Hofmannsthal, Gabriele d'Annunzio and Arthur Machen, as well as contributing articles on philosophy of religion topics to the Ontological Investigations blog. He co-edited *Drowning in Beauty: The Neo-Decadent Anthology* (Snuggly Books, 2018).

MONTAGUE SUMMERS

THE BRIDE
OF CHRIST
and other fictions

edited and with an introduction by
DANIEL CORRICK

THIS IS A SNUGGLY BOOK

ISBN: 978-1-64525-039-5

Contents

Introduction:
Montague Summers
as Seen through His Fiction

A LONG with the preceding volume, *Six Ghost Stories*, this volume brings together the entirety of Montague Summers' known fiction.

To attempt a full or even satisfactory biography of Summers would be futile, both in virtue of his own tendency for mystification and the fact that the majority of the anecdotal resources are still in private hands. It is a task we can only hope some zealous future scholar will undertake. A brief sketch of Summers' life, however, will allow us to explore this individual's fiction in the context of his fascinating and paradoxical character.

Montague Summers was born on the 10th of April, 1880, in Clifton, Bristol. His family was of the Victorian *nouveau riche*, mercantile in origins, Low Church in worship, and somewhat conservative in artistic taste. From a young age he showed great enthusiasm for the theatre along with a mischievous fascination for risqué art and literature, which the family did their best to keep out of his hands. After graduating from Clifton College, Summers went up to Trinity College, Oxford, in 1899, eventually taking a low pass in Theology, followed by an additional three years at Lichfield Theological College in preparation for a placement within the Church of England. During this period, he began to affect a decadent persona, sporting opulent, dandified garb and hinting at sinister occult interests as well as—paradoxically—a recusant devotion to certain medieval saints. In 1908 he began his career as an Anglican deacon. However, Providence or the Devil had other designs. Later that year, Summers and another cleric were suspended from the curacy of Bitton after their failed seduction of a choirboy led to a scandal.

By this time, his spiritual allegiance had drifted so far from Canterbury as to make continued profession of the Anglican creed farcical, so in the absence of material reasons to remain, in the shape of paid placements, he was formally received into the Roman Catholic Church. Sometime at the beginning of the 1910s, he was supposedly ordained as a priest in the same faith. The exact circumstances of this possible appointment were a mystery which Summers himself was at no pains to dispel. Biographical anecdotes suggest it was either undertaken at that time by the "Bishop of Mercia and Middlesex," Vernon Herford, the leader of an ecumenicist group who nevertheless enjoyed clerical legitimacy through his relation to an Eastern Rite Church in communion with Rome, or somewhat later by the then Bishop of Parma and future saint Guido Maria Conforti. Concurrent with this, in keeping with his apparent Jekyll and Hyde tendencies, Summers became active in underground homosexual circles and joined the British Society for the Study of Sex Psychology, then a haven for those with unusual erotic predilections.

As an apparent priest unassigned to a diocese, Summers was forced to earn his living by other means. Here his literary erudition saved him from a number of tedious fates, not the least unappetising of which was the position of Latin master at a London school. With the initial support of Arthur Bullen of the Shakespeare Head Press, he began to compile critical editions of the works of Restoration dramatists, beginning with Aphra Behn and finishing with Thomas Shadwell, and his nemesis John Dryden. An ardent champion of theatre from this period, Summers, in 1919, helped found the Phoenix Society for the Production of Old Plays, which, along with reviving scholarly interest in these works, succeeded in staging many of them, often for the first time in over a century. This new-found literary fame brought him into contact with the renowned critic Edmund Gosse, who was to become a life-long friend, patrons of various London salons, and certain theatrical figures with whom the wayward cleric formed unconventional relationships. Of the latter, one such individual was Hector Stuart-Forbes, a young actor who later became Summers' secretary and helper in old age, and another aspirant actor, Anatole James, who was to be present at an infamous episode in his life.

In 1923, or thereabouts, Summers broke from the homosexual scene he had been periodically involved in, a shadowy subculture where the worlds of ecclesiastics and rent-boys met. He ceased to be involved with the British Society for the Study of Sex Psychology, though he continued to speak highly of its founder, Havelock Ellis. Three years later, he published *The History of Witchcraft and Demonology*. Companion volumes on vampirism, lycanthropy and black magic were soon to follow. Throughout these studies—amalgamations of esoteric history, folklore, ethnography, Church doctrine, and forensic psychology written up in a grand Victorian style—he gleefully affirmed the reality of the phenomena in question, and even hinted at occasional familiarity with them. Unfailingly, they provoked a strong reaction, not only from critics of the paranormal, but also from fellow Catholics embarrassed by reminders of what they saw as the Church's superstitious past.

From the end of the 20s, he turned his attention towards the monstrous in fiction. He compiled three anthologies of ghost stories which were to become classics of the genre, rediscovered several of the "horrid novels" mentioned in Jane Austin's *Northanger Abbey* and long thought her invention, and in 1938 released *The Gothic Quest*, a monumental history of the Gothic Novel which ranks amongst the greatest works the scholarly priest ever produced. Sadly, however, by this point, his relationship with publishers had grown strained. New works would be announced only to slip into oblivion as they were expected to see print. The 40s were not kind to Summers; his health, always delicate, had begun to decline and he found himself forced to write articles for society magazines, a labour in which he took no joy. He spent the last years of his life living quietly in West London with Forbes. On the 10th of August, 1948, a week after informing a friend he'd finished the first volume of his memoirs, he passed away.

After Summers' death, his earthly possessions and the task of handling his literary estate passed on to Hector Stuart-Forbes. Unfortunately, administerial complications meant that Forbes was not immediately able to access the financial legacy and thus was forced to vacate the Richmond home in haste, with only as many of their shared possessions as he could find storage for. His hopes for Summers' work and for vindicating the ecclesiastical status of the latter were to fall short, for his own health had begun to fail, and in 1950 he too passed away. At this point Summers' *Nachlass* was considered lost, either stolen by Forbes' creditors or forgotten in the vaults of some legal firm. In actuality, although some items were misplaced (ironically many of these, such the autobiography *The Galanty Show*, were soon recovered by scholars), most were kept in hand by the solicitors and eventually passed on to Hector's brother Duncan, a Canadian national who carried them back home with him across the Atlantic. In the late 2000s, Duncan's daughter, Betty Harris, uncovered Summers' papers and personal effects and alerted several scholars, including Gerard P. O. Sullivan of Neumann University, who helped arrange the eventual transfer of the papers to the Georgetown University Library Archives.[1]

The rediscovered Forbes collection contained a wealth of unseen materials. Manuscripts of never seen before occult studies, poetry, sketches for future volumes on subjects ranging from crime fiction to the Antichrist, histories of the theatre, correspondence with famous figures, mystical works, notebooks on the Gothic novel and on cases of witchcraft, and a fascinating array of different fictional works.

At first glance one is struck by the extent to which Summers' literary style varied depending on the theme of the work—in true Wildean fashion each stylistic pose is a mask which both superficially hides and tantalisingly reveals something of the author's true personality. That many of the pieces are incomplete or in some cases fragmentary only serves to further emphasise the complexity of his character. Is he an ultra-devout medievalist striving to draw attention to the necessary place of the demonic in Catholic theology or a secret deviant aroused by the thought of evil and sacrilege? A Restoration man of letters reborn armed with rapier-

---

1 For the history of Summers' *Nachlass* following his death I am indebted to Sullivan's own account given in the prologue of the Apocryphile Press edition of *The Vampire: His Kith and Kin*. Gracious thanks must also be rendered to James Jenkins who alerted me to the manuscripts and made the first public announcement of their discovery.

sharp wit and bawdy humour? A languid decadent hymning Hellenic boy-love? A passionate mystic out of touch with the materialism of the age?

His fiction can be divided into roughly four types: ghost stories, Uranian stories, longer society pieces, and the mystical novella "The Bride of Christ," this latter being his most sophisticated and accomplished fictional work. I propose that through an analysis of the recurring themes within these, one can tentatively trace a deeper, underlying theme unifying the multiple aspects of his personality.

The first of the four types, the ghost stories, fall into two categories, the classic and the journalistic. The classic, written very much in the vein of M. R. James and Sheridan le Fanu, make up the contents of *Six Ghost Stories*. In many ways they are a tribute to Summers' favourite fictional reading materials: the Victorian pulps, or "shockers," mentioned so lovingly in *The Galanty Show*, and the old Gothic novels. In the context of his life they represent him at his happiest, being originally written to be read out in the company of friends at Christmas and dealing with subjects he obviously relished, e.g. book collecting and the theatre. From the lengthy introductions included in the anthologies Summers compiled we can also see he attributed a degree of seriousness to the ghost story form, depicting a successful piece as not only the source of authentic (maybe masochistic) pleasure, but also a reminder of "the world invisible" and thence some form of spirituality.

The second category, the journalistic pieces, comprises the ghost stories in this volume, "The Between Maid" and "Ghostly Godstow." In a letter to a prospective publisher for *Six Ghost Stories*, Summers mentioned that he had two further pieces "in germ," which makes one wonder if these were not originally intended for full-length treatment. In any case, "The Between Maid," the only previously published piece in this volume, appeared in a 1945 issue of *Everybody's Weekly*, a frothy middle-class society paper Summers wrote for reluctantly, contributing articles with titles such as "Is Hitler Really Dead?" and "What is a Ghost?" It was accompanied by an illustration by Mervin Peake of *Gormenghast* fame. With this piece Summers succeeds in what he elsewhere deems an almost impossible task—to write a story in which the ghost is an object of pity.

"Ghostly Godstow" takes as its centrepiece an account of the Black Mass. Intriguingly, this part of the plot was inspired by a supposedly factual event which Summers refers to in his *Witchcraft and Black Magic*:

> Not many years previously a black mass was celebrated abominably in the ruins of Godstow Nunnery, and it was with difficulty that an open scandal was averted.

What might be the basis of such an event? Given Summers' notoriously wide definition of black magic, it's hard to imagine a real Satanic coven at work, but might such a report have been inspired by a real ritual, a séance, or a student prank? (Summers lived in Oxford periodically and was well-placed to keep up with gossip, being something of a legend amongst the student population.) The description of the Mass itself—its "scarlet vestments" and "black triangular loafs"—matches that given in *The History of Witchcraft and Demonology*, although the reader will note that the obscene elements so stressed elsewhere are absent, which further suggests the piece was intended for the "polite" readership of *Everybody's Weekly*. Tantalisingly, amongst Summers' papers there are a detailed synopsis and several completed chapters of a book-length study of the Black Mass written at roughly the same period.

The Black Mass theme is a door onto a fascinating and very dark aspect of Summers' character: his extreme interest in the blasphemous. During the first decades of the twentieth century, multiple persons remarked on what his first biographer Brocard Sewell termed a "morbid fascination with evil." When the poet Redwood-Anderson went to visit Summers during the ill-fated Bitton period, he reports on the newly made clergyman subjecting him to a detailed account of the philosophy of Satanism and its rituals, along with the veiled promise of first-hand experience of the same should he desire it. The most disturbing testimony comes from the previously mentioned Anatole James. James, whose real name was Geoffrey Evans Pickering, the alias being initially adopted whilst writing for papers as a ballet critic, was a homosexual adventurer of omnivorous tastes who had been introduced to Summers by Havelock Ellis in view of their shared theatrical interests. According to an account he gave decades later to Timothy d'Arch Smith, Summers performed a Black Mass with James in attendance on Boxing Day, 1918. The exact details are not recorded, but all participants were male and sexual acts were performed. James also claimed to have been Summers' accomplice in the homosexual underground scene, the two meeting at restaurants and thence trawling the streets for male prostitutes together, one such bacchanal leading Summers to confide half-jokingly that he only found pleasure in "the corruption of devout young Catholics." Although that remark was doubtlessly made to shock, both the adventures with James and the recent scandal at Bitton make it apparent that Summers found the utterance and performance of blasphemy titillating.

I cannot agree with the theories considered by Ruben van Luijk in his *Children of Lucifer: The Origins of Modern Religious Satanism*, to the effect that Summers' prime motive for joining the priesthood was the desire to commit blasphemy or to imitate the French novelist J.-K. Huysmans. For one thing, his devotion to High Church causes began very early in life, before any hint of the sinister presented itself. He also put a great deal of energy into his devotional activities before and after his conversion, travelling around Europe to various places of worship, enduring inconvenience and, on some occasions, physical risk. The broader question arises, however: was there a sexual element in his attraction to religion as a whole, and if so what does it mean? One might ask whether he was initially drawn towards Catholicism because of some deeply buried sexual aspect or whether his sexual peculiarities were shaped and informed by his religious tendencies. Summers himself would have found questions of priorities with regards to sexuality and religion ill-founded, however; in his more philosophical moments he suggests that sexuality properly understood lies at the heart of all true religion and that, as it reveals the Divine Immanence, religion encompasses sexuality.

Homosexual Eros, whether explicit or implicit, is the main theme of the three pieces grouped under the heading Uranian: "The Parting of the Ways," "Nocturno Itinere Non Intermisso," and "I Shall in Two Minutes." Of these "The Parting of the Ways" is the only complete story and the most frank discussion of homosexuality anywhere in Summers' writings. Placing it within the context of his literary career presents a challenge; it is difficult to date the manuscript with any degree of accuracy, since it exists only in typescript form without signature or address. The directness of the content implies a pre-1923 date. The fact that it has been typed up suggests both that it was read by another party (Summers hated the typewriter), and that it was intended for publication.

As a work of fiction it encapsulates what Timothy d'Arch Smith, in his brilliant study *Love in Earnest: Some notes on the lives and writings of English "Uranian" poets from 1889 to 1930*, took to be the main thematic concerns of the Uranian movement: the fleeting nature of adolescent beauty, relationships between an educated lover and a working-class but inherently virtuous beloved, the gulf between ideal and reality, and the noble but fundamentally doomed nature of such affections. The setting is Oxford; the protagonist, a student in his final year. The latter embarks on a passionate affair with a baggage handler, which he uses as a case study to illustrate and test his theories on the Greek concept of friendship.

The other two pieces are fragmentary and afford us only the barest glimpse of how their plots might develop beyond the single scene they depict. "Nocturno Itinere non Intermisso" deals with a young student's infatuation, or at least fascination, with his classmate. Of course, the prevalence of homosexual behaviour at public schools and colleges was an open secret even in the pre-war years; amongst Summers' draft manuscripts of what would become *The Galanty Show* there is a short piece, not used in the published work, looking at the "special friendships" that developed between boys at his *alma mater*, Clifton College. Sexual themes are more veiled in the second piece, "I Shall in Two Minutes," which is a dialogue between a youth and his worldly mentor in which the former extols the virtues of a life spent embracing every experience, moral and immoral. It is obviously patterned on Lord Henry Wotton's conversation with the titular character in *The Picture of Dorian Gray*.

Oxford was the cradle of the Uranian movement; there were its first major voices heard in periodicals such as *The Spirit Lamp*, Alfred Lord Douglas's magazine, and *The Chameleon*, which sealed the fate of Oscar Wilde. Although Summers arrived too late to contribute to any of the major publications, something of its spirit survived in artistic circles, particularly those sympathetic to the more lush style of poetry. The only other discussion of Uranian love from Summers' pen is an essay entitled "A Platonic Idyll," ostensibly a review of Forest Reid's *The Garden God*, but really a somewhat predictable paean to "love beyond the love of women," written in the most youthfully artificial perfumed prose. Despite a certain jaundiced beauty to these pieces, one feels Summers was never able to develop or fully integrate a Uranian ideal with the rest of his personality and outlook: unlike fellow Catholics John Gray and Marc-André Raffalovich, he does not attempt to synthesise homosexual love with Christian anthropology, nor does he propose it as the basis for a Neo-Hellenistic Brotherhood of Man.

The pieces one might label, for want of a better term, "society stories," i.e. "Barbara Marsham" and "In Spite of the Fitful Promise," are both opening chapters to longer works Summers never completed. In the first, the protagonist, a materialistic but dissatisfied woman with an equally venal mother, comes under pressure to marry her boorish step-brother lest she lose access to an inheritance. The second deals with the matriarch of a cathedral town and the stuffy tea-table politics she engages in for want of anything better to occupy her time. Both pieces are written in an elegant, lyrical prose style at odds with their seemingly trivial subject matter. There is an element of literary as well as social satire at work too: given both feature high-ranking Anglican ecclesiastics who are anything but spiritual, the novels of Anthony Trollope (who Summers found insufferable) might well be their target.

The deeper theme to both is repression, both personal and sexual. The protagonists live a stultifying existence enlivened only by the petty politics of their parochial social sets, ruthlessly suppressing any thoughts of "romantic nonsense" or other non-utilitarian concerns. One suspects that the introduction of the eccentric, even mystically inclined Catholic character in "Barbara Marsham" is intended as a counter-point to such bourgeois venality. Like many homosexual writers of the period, Summers shows considerable interest in and sympathy for feminine sexuality.

This brings us to that final, unique work: "The Bride of Christ." At once the most decadent and the most Catholic of all Summers' writings, it tells of an English convent of Mercedarian nuns whose way of life is threatened by their new confessor, Father Cassilis, a theological modernist who considers their form of mystical devotion superstitious and hysterical. Central to this conflict is a young nun, Sister Veronica, whose devotional practices had hitherto brought her to states of mystical ecstasy as the Beloved of the Divine Bridegroom, and who now finds her faith assailed on all sides by doubts, metaphysical and romantic. The story is told in a fugue of dream reveries and smouldering lyrical prose reminiscent of the French Symbolists. One major model for its plot is George Moore's 1905 novel, *Sister Teresa*, which deals with a penitent noviticate's struggles against both her own sensuality and the lure of heretical pantheism.

Summers praises *Sister Teresa* as a "fine, almost unique novel" in the *Galanty Show*, though cautions that it captures nothing of the interior life, the soul of the convent, intimating—one now feels—that he himself could do so. Had he managed to publish "The Bride of Christ" then the world would have seen him amply justified in that claim. There is ambiguity over whether or not this novella is complete, with Sullivan arguing for its incompleteness on the basis of its lacking a colophon page, although this might be due to Summers' not having prepared the manuscript for circulation among potential publishers. As it stands, the final lines close the narrative in a starkly effective manner, giving it a sense of poetic emphasis Moore's lacks.

Absent from Moore's novel and central to Summers' is the symbolism of the mystical marriage, a favourite theme of the great mystics of the Spanish Golden Age, St. John of the Cross and St. Teresa of Avila. Depicting union with God as union with the beloved has a long history in the Abrahamic religions dating back at least to the Song of Solomon, however, many nineteenth-century theologians were uncomfortable with its sexual implications, not least because of the vogue amongst atheist critics for using implied sexual readings to delegitimise religious discourse. It is the sexual aspects of this bridal theology that Summers emphasises throughout, the language used to describe visions and dreams being positively orgasmic in nature. With this in mind, Father Cassilis's condemnation of Veronica's mystic practices represents not so much a clash between theological modernism and traditionalism as between the "suspicious" modern mind-set, which sees any heightened display of sexual emotion—especially on the part of women—as evidence of a pathology, and a tradition which is avowedly sexual in its symbolism. One feels that he is close to invoking the names of Freud and Charcot and the charge of "hysteria." As the Spanish mystics faced persecution from the Inquisition on one side, and social pressures of marriage on the other, so Veronica is assailed by this sceptical scrutiny and aching memories of worldly love. Ultimately hers is not just a battle to retain personal faith against sceptical suspicion, but also a struggle for the legitimacy of sensual mysticism.

By way of conclusion to this analysis I would like to suggest that Veronica's battle is to an extent the author's own. The deeper theme throughout Montague Summers' life and writings is the presence of sexuality at the heart of the spiritual discourse. It's not for nothing that his final work was on the bodily manifestations of mystical ecstasy. Even given the fashions of the time, it is unsurprising he would be drawn towards Catholicism, for that religion places great emphasis on physicality; unlike the fundamental direction of Protestantism, in which salvation is sought through an interior affirmation of faith, the Roman creed affirms salvation through bodily devotions, the utterance of liturgical rites, symbolic ornamentation in clothing and architecture, the pressing of the lips to funerary relics and, at its heart, the consumption of the very flesh and blood of God in the Eucharist. For someone like Summers, whose approach to mysticism was sensual rather than intellectual, it offers a form of worship covering the whole range of the senses, including the erotic. Homosexual eros, though, has relatively few opportunities for expression within orthodox Catholicism, save for in the cultus of certain boy saints. Given the influence of the Decadents and Summers' love of theatricality, it is perhaps not surprising that at one time he sought this erotic expression in Catholicism's dark mirror, Diabolism. From a psychological perspective, his brief flirtation with Satan should be seen as a Jungian *Nigredo* phase by which he reached a greater consciousness of the divine through an exploration of his own darker aspects. Thence he approached the world through a more morally charged Catholic voluptuousness, both through condemnation of daemonic carnality and through exhalation of the passion of the saints. In terms of literature, at least, it may be that with "The Bride of Christ" he at last found a way to express his eroticised vision of spirituality through the medium of the female psyche.

—Daniel Corrick

A Note on the Texts

OUT of the pieces collected together in this volume, only one, "The Between Maid," which appeared in the January 3rd 1948 issue of *Everybody's Weekly*, has previously seen publication. All the other materials originated from the Montague Summers papers: Box 3, Folder 8, Georgetown University Library, Booth Family Center for Special Collections, Washington D.C. In the case of those pieces where a formal title was lacking, the first words of the piece have been used for the title. A more thorough breakdown of their origins is as follows:

The text of "The Bride of Christ" is taken from a 62 page manuscript (complete with title page) with an earlier 11-page draft used to check certain phrases. It might interest readers to know that Summers initially intended his heroine to go by the decidedly decadent name of Salomé.

"Nocturno Itinere non Intermisso" originates from a 5-page manuscript written in very faint pencil. "In Spite of the Fitful Promise" is from an 11-page, hand-written manuscript. "The Parting of the Ways" is taken from a 12-page typescript. "Barbara Marsham" is an amalgamation of two manuscripts, an early draft of 14 pages and a more developed 15-page rewrite of the first chapter. "I Shall in Two Minutes" comes from a 4-page manuscript, the pages numbered 27 to 30, meaning that it was certainly part of a longer work. "Ghostly Godstow" exists both in manuscript and typescript form (each 5 pages), the former of which bears Summers' Hove address, further confirming it was written around the same time as *Six Ghost Stories*.

It was Summers' wont to make substantial revisions over the course of a single manuscript, meaning that a certain degree of editorial interpretation is necessary to make sense of the mass of marginalia, deletion and additions; in cases where there is no clear indication of which amendments he preferred, decisions have been made on the basis of readability and, on occasion, legibility.

The publisher and editors would like to thank the staff at the Archives for their invaluable assistance and support, especially Ted Jackson without whom this volume would not have been possible.

Editorial thanks is also due to Roger Dobson and Timothy d'Arch Smith for their advice back in the day and to Quentin S. Crisp for his proof-reading acumen on the introduction.

THE BRIDE
OF CHRIST
and other fictions

The Bride of Christ

Your aching eyelids faint
In this pretence of chastity,
The mystic spousal that shall be
Betwixt your Lord and you . . .
. . . .
Eyelids heavy with the sense
Of some strange passionate suspense,
And your mouth subtly hungering
Who knows for what forbidden thing?
—*Arthur Symons.*

I

THE sun, weary of the hot listless day, was slowly beginning to fade towards a west that burned all crimson fire and tawny gold, and the trees were casting their slant shadows longer and darker over the kempt lawns

It was a quaint old garden, full of gay coloured flowers with rustic names, oxlips, shepherd's gipsciere, columbines, perse and red: nor were there lacking sage and mint, valerian, sorrel, with all the plants that make an ancient herbary.

The low box too that fringed each wall was cut at the corners into fantastic shapes, peacocks, chanticleers, or again cockerels and finials, as though fashioned by the hand of some hedgerow architect.

A great peace and tranquillity lay over the garden like a mystic veil, a calm intensified by the approach of evening. It seemed the pleasance of the palace of the sleeping maiden in nursery lore, courts where nobody has trod for an hundred years, whose silence has been broken by no voice, whose flowers have never been plucked by intrusive hands, yet which, in the magic of their ensorcellment, remains ever the same, wonderful and beautiful, awaiting the advent of the prince.

Indeed one could almost imagine that he was soon to start forth from the coppice, a gallant boy; sword in hand, breaking through the briars, scaling the high walls, a lad with love-light in his eyes, and the warm kiss on his eager lips.

Meanwhile, the garden waited.

But no fond fairy prince ever came there: the ramparts were very tall, perhaps too tall for him, and the huge iron gates at the end of the winding drive had long been fast, clasped with a giant padlock, grown rusty and stubborn in idleness.

The house was stolidly builded and planned. In spite of many additions and alterations, the oratory, offices, the squat cloister with its garth, it retained a square Georgian aspect, for the main pavilion indeed had been erected in the days of Anne and her successor when Hampstead was true country unlinked to London town.

The supplements, however, had largely detracted from a tendency to mere lumpish mass, and even lent it a straggling air which became almost bizarre, greatly enhanced by the elaborate frontage of the chapel with its obvious cupola and surmounting gilt cross.

Aesthetically such an extension left much to be desired, and yet the baroque building was not without charm, due to its very quaintness, brown and sober with age. Moreover, the garden in itself demanded those stout stone pillars, the heavy corniced porch, the immense doors opening centrally, obviously no longer so used, since in one of them had been made a wicket for the service of the inmates. Corroded and weatherworn, there still could be seen a ring for the linksman's torch, long since idle now, but the old knockers had been wrenched away, though rusty rivets and clamps marked where once it hung.

This, formerly the main entrance to the house, had for many a year been deposed in place of a smaller, a mere postern in the wall which rounded the south side, whence strangers could gain admittance to the chapel by passing from the public lane along a gravel path boarded with privet to the left, completely screened off from the rest of the building and thence only to be reached through a door, which, perpetually locked, in the course of time naturally closed over with a thick growth of lush ivy and Virginian creeper, rarely, if ever, cleared.

As the sun died and the equivocal dusk of evening crept up, suffusing the landscape with undecided mauve, with blues and grey, hybrid, epicene, such an evening as that when Watteau's company had embarked for languorous Cythera, surely one, not perhaps wholly rapt in a dream of the past, might have heard the patter of high-heeled shoes and the flou-flou of a rustling skirt across the terraces and have seen gay gentlemen in their satin breaches with coats of plum velvet and purple bow before the powdered dark-eyed coquette, toying so daintily with her pretty painted fan, and, while they lightly flick the fallen snuff-grains from mechlin and valenciennes, surely one might hear their voices, albeit etiolated and wan, vow and protest that she was monstrous handsome.

In such a spot and at such an hour, evoked by the witchery of an evening which melts reality into reverie, even yet some phantom Careless with his Lady Betty Modish, Clarinda and Plume may enact an unwritten scene of Cibber or Vanbrugh, making love with much sparkle and effervescent wit; if not entirely in earnest, at least not altogether in jest. But were we to look too close they would mingle, poor fantoches, with the empty night, and what we deemed the flutter of a gown is but the shadow of a tree quivering in some passing breeze, the glint of diamond buckles but the brilliance of the dew upon the lawn.

They have flitted by to mope and murmur on the other boards and left the stage clear to play our parts, which we do, most of us, not so gracefully.

She stood upon the ancient terrace, gazing out over the garden with its flowers and lawns bounded by thickets and green shrubbery, but her wistful eyes saw much more than what lay so immediately before her. Nor was it altogether the memory of a haunting past that woke itself there, but rather that dim dumb longing not unmixed with weariness and a strange sad pain, which we see in the look of some faithful animal that has learned to love, and is noble beyond his kind.

The sunset and its iridescent aureole, its rage and glory like the pyre burned when a mighty Viking dies; the new moon a crescent just risen, clean and luminous in the soft sky, beneath whose nether horn, seemingly held by a silver thread, there shone one radiant star; the fragrance and beauty of the night sighing among the tall tree tops, all held nothing for her, such fairness could not wean her from the thoughts which possessed her soul, nor print one swift emotion on her pallid face.

She stood motionless and alone.

So white, so wan, were her countenance and the waxen hands muffled in full wide sleeves, that they appeared hardly distinguishable from the creamy folds of the habit itself, from the spotless swathing of the ample scapular, which fell loosely over her shoulders to the bare sandaled feet, and whereon, just over the heart, there gleamed, printed in rouge and or, the historic badge of Jamye el Conquistador, four pallets, and in chief a cross pattée.

Even the long rosary of fifteen decades and the cross on which agonised a silver Christ were virgin white: the black veil over a linen wimple added but a new transparency to the thin cheeks, only on the left side the Augustinian girdle hung far down, a narrow slip of blank leather.

And upon the fourth finger of her left hand was the dull glitter of a gold circle.

For she was a bride, wedded to a Spouse, who, although unseen they might be, was more exacting than any husband of Earth: although invisible for a while, fidelity to Him was no easy task, since the lightest look, a touch, a thought, might all be treachery to this Bridegroom who seems to ask so much. And He asks so much, because His love, His desire, is so great.

As she mediated, the beauty of the gloaming with its gracious gift of peace inevitably entered into her soul, and the Divine Desire, eager, febrile, engulfed her in its embrace like a veil, like a sweet yet potent perfume poured about the very circumference of the air. In such silent solitary communion with nature the permeation of God's presence expressed itself to her invincible force. Everything was full of, effervescent with, that mystic power, which drew her by an overwhelming magnetism of spirit and intoxicated her with its fragrancy.

No effort upon her part was needed. There were many who strained sleepless nights and broken days after God: she herself had groped for dateless hours, which seemed an eternity and a hell, striving, and He had not been found. Yet when the soul remained passive without prayer and yearning, suddenly He was there, and the whole being woke at His advent.

It was a sort of Quietism. The patient was thrown, inert and resistless, into the infinite, and then, through time and space, annihilating everything, yet rendering the soul exquisitely sensible, came this spasm, the thrill which almost mounted to an ecstasy. There was no effort, no call, no cry, only nothing save waiting, blindly, aimlessly, which was the hardest of all.

The nun had been walking in the garden, and before entering the house, she turned once more to look at the flowers she dared to love, not wholly forgetful it might be of the Master's injunction, who bade us consider even the lilies how they grow, and she loitered a few moments upon the old grey terrace.

The garden with its sleepy flowers was for her a source of never-failing delight, and she thought of the pantheists with their subtle philosophy which catches the heart in a web meshed of fine gold whose bait is so vast a truth that it soothly seems the whole.

They are there from all the ages, a mighty band, and their eyes are beautiful with verities, thin lips red and lovely with the fairness of their speech; poets and seers, their brows are girded with laurel, their mouths curved with immortal song, but in their hearts lies an eternal sorrow. Never-the-less they tell of wonderful things, and they sing how God is in the acorn and in the wind, in the apple-blossom, in the ripe grapes and in the silver spray of the sea. "God is all and all is God!" And to one looking upon the dawn, upon the sunlight over the infinite ripples of blue water, to one who stands girt with the everlasting silence that habits among the crest of great mountains, who shall say if false be their rede?

What matters if they be of Greece and of India, of mystic Persia or mediaeval Germany? The same are the maxims of Krishna enunciating that he is both worshipper and worshipped, moisture in the water, light in the planets, human nature in man, as the precepts of the contemplative Angelus who cried "Cannot do without God nor He without me; He is as small as I, and I as great as He!"

The perfume of attar is sweet in the rose gardens, where amorous bulbucks love to linger long; the moon, a jewel clasped in night's dark bosom, shines white above sable cypress and sycamores; a hundred fountains plash drops of crystal rain, and there we hear Hafiz singing to the mistralry of crisp tinkling tambourines and voluptuous dulcimers how that he would freely give all Samarkand and Bukhārā town for the tiny mole on the soft cheek of his minion; and anon when they are come to tell him of the doing to death of Mansur al-Hallaj, who had too boldly proclaimed "I am the Truth," the poet, ceasing not from his dalliance, replies "He should not have revealed the mystery."

Upon some vast savannah beneath the Southern Cross, Walt Whitman, sitting it may be by the bivouac's fitful flame, his arm falling around the neck of his tan-faced prairie boy, who gave more than all the gifts of the world, lifted his titan voice in the creed:

I hear and behold God and every object,
    yet understand God not in the least
Nor do I understand who there be more
    wonderful than myself.
. . . . . . Without me what were all? what
were God?

God created Earth as well as heaven, and when He looked, beheld it was very good. Francis of Assisi, the wanderer about the Tuscan byways told us something of this, and men have loved him for it ever since.

And so they ask us if God is to be found more intimately in that thin white wafer, which macabre monks elevate and adore, than in the virgin calix of an arum lily with its lovely golden spear, so delicate, so fragrant, so pure; if the Eternal Voice speaks not as plain in the soughing of the west wind or the majesty of the cyclone, as in the ritual mutter of the mass and the thunder of organs orgulous at some high festival?

Long centuries before man was convicted of sin, before the call of Yahweh had been heard crying aloud in Paradise, paganism, fair and young, vested all nature with a life that was visible, even tangible.

There were satyrs in the woods, and fauns, brown boys with furry ears and wide slanted eyes, there were dryads, hamadryades, nymphs of the forest and the stream, undines for the water, sylphs for the air. Greater than these are Pan, the omnipotent force of nature; Demeter, mystical sovereign of the yellow corn-crop about whose wan brow clung the red petals of poppy; her daughter pale Persephone; Pomona, who smiled when the orchards ripened at the fading of summertide; Flora, fragrant with flowers, and a thousand more. These were gods for the sheepcote and the lyre, gods for the hill and the plain, for the heath and the wine, friendly, helpful, grateful for sacrifice and rustic sacrament.

They were the poetry of the world.

But the antiphonal chant of the black-robed sons of Basil and the cowled Benedict has stayed the music of the oaten pipes. The melody was stilled and drowned in sad liturgies, its dancers are all fled away.

There are beautiful stories of the old cenobites, of Anthony and Hilarion, dwellers in Libanus and the Thebaid.

One aged solitary, journeying far out over the desert, met in his path a strange creature, gentle and timid withal, a lad having little horns upon his head and the hooves of a goat. And recognising that he was a faun, stayed for a space from his kind, the hermit spoke courtesy to him, and broke bread, for he knew that all creatures are verily of one Father. And as he departed on his way the old man blessed the stranger.

Great was their simplicity, and great their love.

"Wilt thou yet take all, Galilean? but these
    thou shalt not take,
The laurel, the palms and the pæan, the
    breasts of the nymphs in the brake;
Breasts more soft than a dove's . . . . . ."

She started. It was almost as if a low insistent voice had sighed the words in her ear, and the haunting of the rhythm came back across a little gulf of time.

Trouble gathered in her eyes, No! The garden was no longer lovely. It was all grey and shadowy, a monochrome and dusk. It was full of temptation.

The nun crossed herself hurriedly, almost in fear. Such songs were not for her, and as she made the sacred sign, another phrase heard that morning in the refectory intervened, and the calm set tones of the reader lulled the premonition in her heart. "The love of things created is deceitful and inconsistent: the love of Jesus is faithful and constant."

Deceitful! That was it! Deceitful! How wise of heart, how very wise holy Thomas à Kempis was!

And as she turned with bended head toward the door, the Angelus rang out close and clear in the still evening.

"Ecce ancilla Domini, Fiat mihi secundum verbum tuum."

II

The Celestial, Royal, and Military Order of Our Lady of Mercy for the Redemption of Captives was founded in accordance with the direct command of Madonna, given to Peter Nolasco.

In Languedoc he had often heard John de Matha preaching the deliverance of Christian prisoners from

Moorish dungeons, and upon the first of August, 1218, at Barcelona, as he was reciting office in choir, the Immaculate Virgin, crowned with golden stars and clad in white robes of dazzling purity, appeared to him, and holding forth a snowy scapula bade him institute an Order whose aim should be the liberation of captives from the infidel, for which end the brothers themselves must not hesitate cheerfully to deliver their own bodies in exchange for the ransom of slaves: in the same night she was also seen of Peter's director, Raymond of Penyafort, a holy Dominican, and of Don Jamye of Aragon, by whose substantial aid the foundation was accomplished.

Under the protection of the Mother of Mercy, honoured in every house as principle Patron and heavenly foundress, whose festival is most solemn and most stately of the long liturgical cycle, the new Order flourished apace. Although in their days wholly religious, at its birth many knights and grandees were enrolled in its ranks, and when Peter Nolasco, worn out with penitence and works, expired at midnight one Christmas Eve, murmuring with his latest breath, "The Lord hath sent redemption unto His people," it had spread widely, and was firmly planted throughout Spain, even extending far and finding warm welcome in other lands.

Very early in the history of the Order, Maria de Cervellon, the wealthy daughter of a noble house, became the first Mercedarian nun, and, at Barcelona, opened convents for women to ally themselves to the Fathers of Redemption.

Contemplative, observing strict enclosure, it is their part to pray unceasingly, to meditate, to apply their fasts and austerities, the fruit of starven vigil, their disciplines and tears, to the general good.

In 1265 there were also installed Tertiaries, who could labour manually and beg alms from door to door.

Hundreds of miserable captives were redeemed, hundreds of white-robed religious languished in the noisome prisons of sultan and bashaw.

The Order blushed red with the blood of many martyrs, of Serapion, an English lad, who lashed to a cross and tortured, ceasing never to exclaim "Deliver not unto the brute beasts the souls of them that trust in Thee," until they severed his neck with a scimitar, and his soul flew to cry aloud with those under the mystic altar of the Apocalypse.

In the shadow of the flower-like Alhambra, a caliph butchered Peter Pascasio, Bishop of Jaén: they hanged Peter Armengol from a tree, so that for the rest of his life his neck was twisted and writhen, his gaze ever livid with the agony.

And whilst the fathers and brothers went out rejoicing to the arid sands and foul cities of Barbary, there to fall to the moslem's yataghan, or, worser fate, to live on, slaves, through hideous days beneath the lurid glare of an unwinking sun, that scorched and stirred up all the loathsome and leprous stench of oriental slums, verminous and vile; in Madrid, among the dark dim cloisters and cell of a remote convent, Marianna di Gesù was performing incredible penances, passing whole hours and months of such frantic pain and agony, that the brief moments when she gave, what was for her, respite to her bleeding body and tormented nerves, seemed to others the acme of a martyrdom most dolorous

It was no easy rule that of the Mercedari, it is no light life nor vainly to be undertaken.

However, as the time went on, and the very object for which it was primarily founded in so especial a manner passed entirely away, becoming a mere historical circumstance of the past, when the green standards and gold crescent of the Prophet were rolled back from the Peninsula, his pride humbled and his people cabined more and more by the victorious West: this great Order, once so widely spread over Christendom, but at length decimated by the very accomplishment of its end, torn by internal dissensions, wounded by the general decline of monasticism, harassed by those of a new era that proved pregnant with free thought, with humanism, with licence and anti-monarchism, rapidly languished and began to fade and decay.

So in these later centuries the Mercedari, robbed of their purpose by time and change, their ancient prestige vanished in the midst of a social condition long since obsolete, have dwindled and are fallen into unwonted obscurity.

In Spain, their natal land, there are yet many convents, men and women. The fathers have a province in the Argentine Republic: they are popular in South America, in Spanish colonies, and those countries where Spanish influence predominates.

In Rome the one house adjoins the church of S. Adriano which occupies the site of the Curia built by Tullus Hostilius upon the spot that story points to as the first meeting-place of Tatius and the traitress Tarpeia. Where Patres Conscripti once sat in solemn senate, here sons of Mary Merciful, a goddess unknown to primal Rome, chant the praises of their Queen.

III

At the time of the publication of the bull *Universalis Ecclesiae* and the subsequent restatement of the hierarchy of England, there lived in semi-retirement near London a Spanish widow who possessed a large income and the well-preserved remains of considerable beauty.

Famously a mistress of Manuel Godoy, although unacknowledged for fear of royal jealousy, she had in her later years supplanted the passion of love with that of religion. By no very difficult psychological process her favourites were turned into saints, the lips that had lingered long upon the young mouth of Eloy de Cristóbal now chastely kissed a relic of Vincente Ferrer.

This soon put her in the highway of dauntless fanaticism, and she gained a considerable reputation for piety. The energy once expended upon statecraft and intrigue was accordingly directed to spiritual liaisons and the politics of heaven, and if she bestowed the fervour upon her prayers she had been wont to give her billets-doux, no doubt they obtained for her a high place in paradise.

A zelatrix intensely concerned in the renewal of religious life in England, the idea occurred to her to devote her money to the formation of a Spanish foundation, so that she might find a small oasis, as it were, of her land in an alien country, and with this object in view she purchased an estate at Hampstead, which had just been vacated by a community of Bernardines, settled there some seventy-years before, but then just removing to a larger and more commodious house.

Desiring an Order completely Spanish she wrote the prioress of the Convent of Enclosed Mercedarians at Burgos, where as a girl she had herself been educated among the sisters, and placed the building at their absolute disposal, further pledging herself at death to endow the nuns with the whole of her fortune without an exception.

At first difficulties arose, but when Cardinal Wiseman, eager for the restoration of contemplatives, warmly seconded the request, the Mother's hesitation was speedily overcome and a company of ten sisters with a duly selected and consecrated supervisor soon took up their residence at Hampstead.

Delighted at the success of her plans, the widow lavished gifts upon the newcomers, and the chapel of the Order was furnished in the richest style, every ornament, every vestment however being indispensably brought from Spain itself, owing to which method the house acquired and presented a completely continental appearance and atmosphere. The very stained glass, replacing the frosted windows which had sufficed the simple Bernardines, came from a dismantled monastery at Córdova.

Day after day, at earliest mass, at every office, the aged Devotee knelt before the curved screen that separated the choir from the public portion, a striking figure, clad in sombre black robes, stiff and statuesque, her snowy hair covered with the graceful mantilla she had never abandoned.

And then one morning she was not seen in her usual place. Before the week was out dirges and requiems were sung. Dying in the habit of the Order of Redemption, she was, by a special indult, buried in the cloistral cemetery, a tiny plot, the mound marked but by an iron cross, nameless and humble.

IV

The Convent of Our Lady of Mercy and S. James had in the course of sixty years obtained its full quota of English novices. Occasionally a French or Spanish postulant was received: in one case the daughter of an ambassador joined the Order, but the generality of the recruits were British.

The cloisters and garth which had once known but the syllables of that tongue, wherein, as quaint old Howell has it, God Almighty surely created the universe, gradually accustomed themselves to the more strenuous sound of Northern speech. Only as some older nuns, the original inhabitants, paced the garden walks or gossiped discretely in the summer-house would listening blossoms and trees hear again the flurry of languid words that seemed to have caught in their parlance some fair ray of sunlight, some beauty as of Moorish arabesques.

The years rolled on, and of the first sisters, a few, repeatedly attacked by rheumatisms and bronchitis, had been compelled to return to their own warm south: a few had passed beyond, their places being filled by fresh faces: a few remained, the Prioress, Mother Asuncion Vera, and some three more, very ancient and feeble of gait.

Yet the traditions of the Order were maintained, without relaxation or change.

After the death of their patroness, they had none to represent their interests, and they began to fall into the background.

Although there was never any continued and serious lack of novices, a fact probably owing to the littleness of the house, yet on the other hand there was never any remarkable increase, nothing to justify the expectation of growth or expansion. Now and again a retreat was held at the convent, but even they became more and more infrequent. The prioress, never perhaps quite forgetting her diffidence as a stranger, was loath to push the interests of the community or arrogate to it any prominent place.

English Benedictines and Dominicans of the Third Order, Ursulines and the Congregations active or semi-enclosed, completely overshadowed this world of foreign foundation. There are no friars of Our Lady of Ransom in England.

For all its gifts and loveliness, days often passed without an exterior entering their chapel; only on Sunday mornings at early mass Catholics from the houses in the nearer neighbourhood, girls in domestic service, and a few Irish, would occasionally assist.

The later mass was sung by the nuns for the nuns alone.

The question of completely closing the chapel to the public had been often mooted, only it was felt that such a step would not be strictly in accordance with the wishes of their foundress; that no expense and that little labour was entailed, that it was doubtless a boon to the handful who did attend, and moreover in the summer strangers were often seen at the afternoon Benediction.

The house was wealthy but utterly obscure.

V

There was silence, and in the pause the papers rustled crisply under the old woman's hand as she turned them over mechanically, half-unconsciously, gazing at the thin white glass before her, in which the grey eyes underlined and ringed by violet shadows, seemed to burn as with a fever.

She was perplexed and disconnected. It was hard to know what to say next, and as she cast about for words which should neither be trivial nor decisive her wrinkled fingers still played aimlessly with the letters and leaflets.

The Prioress was sitting at her writing-desk, a large table which stood somewhat in one corner, so that she faced the door, whilst behind her there was only the plastered wall, upon which, just over her head, hung in an eighteenth-century copy a gaunt and realistic "Monk at Prayer" of Zurbarán

It was a large long room, and this bright-morning the sun poured in through the French windows that opened out on to the terrace. Uncarpeted, save for a dark and well-worn strip where the Prioress sat, the boards were strained, and here and there lay a thick rug.

The mantelpiece which rose almost to the ceiling was a marvellous piece of woodwork, the work of some emulator of Grinling Gibbons.

The hearth was tiled with old Dutch squares on which gaudy cherubim puffing out fat faces, and plethoric patriarchs wearing huge full-bottomed periwigs, enacted the more violent scenes from the Old Testament. Joshua in jack-boots was issuing command to a peevish moon and a surprised looking sun with human countenances; next to him in a wonderful perspective of palms, wives and domestics, Moses, hampered by a voluminous flowered toga, was receiving two enormous tablets of stone from clouds like feather-beds; and in another place the chief incident of his childhood was signified by the appearance of Pharaoh's daughter as a buxom vrow in a towered head, light-laced stays and a petticoat with prinked lapels.

A deep recess, the fireplace was furnished with dogs and andirons, massive and heavy. They burned wood and pinecones there when the weather was frosty.

In the centre of the broad shelf above, flanked by a couple of sconced candles, stood a Spanish image of the Madonna, a waxen doll, robed in black velvet and gold, through whose heart struck a great silver sword. On either end a watercolour sketch was placed. The painting to the right represented the Puerta de Santa Maria at Burgos, the other the vast and lovely Charterhouse of Miraflores.

There were several chairs, some pushed back, so that the first impression was that of bareness. They were merely cane seats, although the Mother herself used a Glastonbury chair of dark oak with scrolls and inscriptions, and there were besides two capacious leathern fauteuils.

The walls were naked save for three or four canvases, sacred subjects, old and dim.

In one corner was suspended a large crucifix, beneath which stood an ancient and unwieldy prie-dieu. Hard by, a holy-water stoup with a sprig of hyssop was affixed to the wall.

There were books everywhere, on the tables, on the chairs, even ledgers and folios piled on the floor. A large bunch of flowers was a note of colour and lightness in a gay blue china bowl by the window.

"Believe me, Veronica, I quite appreciate your difficulties. But you ask me to act so suddenly and that is just what I cannot do."

"Oh, Mother," she replied; clasping and unclasping her hot hands in hectic eagerness, "if you would only . . ."

The cold level tones of the Prioress, tones utterly sexless as are ever the voices of those who have dwelt long in retreats, secluded from the world, broke in upon the hasty-gasping accents of the pleading nun.

"My dear child, you must be content to be patient. I know how easy to preach, how hard to practise the doctrine of patience is. But that is one of our lessons; what we are here especially to learn. And some are taught in one way, some in another."

"I am not here to do anything but to love Christ!" exclaimed the nun impetuously, "and I feel that Father Cassilis is an impediment to me, a stumbling-block. Oh, I cannot confess to him any more!"

"Hush, you hardly know what you are saying. I freely admit that Father Cassilis is not the type of priest who suits us entirely, who understands . . . our temperament, our objects even, shall I say? But there can be no doubt he is a very estimable character. He performs his every duty with scrupulous punctuality."

"I cannot see that he does more than a paid chaplain ought to do. A mere secular priest . . ."

"You are excited, child, or you would not talk like this. I sympathise with you; your difficulties are to a large extent mine also; they are common to us all. Our chaplain is not in touch with us. Yet we cannot say that it is his fault. It is an unfortunate circumstance, but you grieve me very much when you speak harshly as you do."

"Cannot you write, Reverend Mother, to His Eminence or Monsignor Kepell and ask for him to be replaced? I am sure there dozens of missions where Father Cassilis would do good work. Surely religious should be served by a religious."

The Prioress sighed. "Ah, yes, there you touch the core of the whole matter. Yet we have generally been fortunate in that respect. But I can remember, many years ago, we had as now a secular chaplain. He did not remain long, but a few months sufficed to show how unsuited an arrangement it was, and we were all, I think, glad when he left."

"Just so, and it will be the same thing over again. Nor am I alone, I am sure that all the Sisters feel just the same as I do, and as for Mother Aña . . ."

"Has Mother Aña said anything to you on the subject?"

"No, Mother, but I can tell that she is unhappy from the way she looks and acts. I know what is wrong."

"It is very indiscreet of you to indulge in such surmises. If anyone has cause for complaint she will doubtless confide the vexation to me. Nobody, save yourself, Veronica, has yet done so, and I have no reason to suppose that anybody will. We must accept these crosses, as God sends them. Did we always experience lively faith, were we ever under the guidance of those who sensibly lead us by the hand, we should be too happy. No doubt we shall gain as much, though in a different way and one not so agreeable to ourselves, from Father Cassilis' ministrations as we used to do from those of Don Bartholomew. The archbishop is, I know, at the present time overpressed with business. There are the burning questions of Catholic schools, and many another. Father Cassilis has only been with us five months, and I feel I cannot ask for his removal without some very definite and valid reason. Were you all to unite in one general and unanimous petition, a . . ." here she hesitated a moment, "a round robin—is not that right?—it would be my duty to consider it most seriously. Even then I doubt if I could act immediately. I will go as far as to say were I to consult my feelings, my private wishes, an alteration would be made."

"But, Mother, can you assert that our chaplain is actively good for the community?"

"Good—good—that is such a vague term. I am convinced that he is an excellent man in his way, although, as I have allowed, unsuitable for us. Yet this very difference may be beneficial to our life. Unless instant occasion demands I shall not interfere until Monsignor's visit, when I shall lay the affair fully before him in confidence. But I am talking too much. Pray be satisfied to know that for the present, at any rate, matters must be left as they are."

"Monsignor's visit! Perhaps not till after Christmas!"

"My dear daughter, I have considered the matter from every point of view. You are only looking at it from one side."

"Don Bartholomew was directly leading me to the acme of joy. He understood. He was a true mystic . . . he encouraged . . . he advised."

"Well, you must now be content to walk without leaning overmuch on a staff. Summon your own strength: the path is the same finally."

"If he were only leading me rightly!"

"It is impossible that the guidance of well-intentioned director should not lead you rightly even though it may seem hard and difficult. There is no use in continuing this conversation. Unless, my child, you with to speak to me on other matters it concludes here. I beg you will not reopen the topic again." With these words the Prioress turned to her papers, and the sunlight lit a violet flame of beauty as it touched the purple life of the amethyst that gleamed on her finger. Her action was a token of dismissal, but the nun fell back in her chair, ghastly pale.

"Then I shall lose my soul!" she moaned in a hollow voice.

The old woman rose to her feet hurriedly, her long white scapular sending a flight of leaves to the floor where they lay unregarded like monstrous flakes of snow. "I cannot make you understand—you do not realise what it means to me," murmured Veronica in a strangled sob, "you think that I am excitable, foolish, because I beg—I implore you to change our confessor. But I tell you, Mother, that Father Cassilis is killing my soul. I am losing the grace of God. What an awful thing it would be if one were to incur not absolution but hell and damnation through a sacrament! I am the bride of Christ! O! That is one thing I always cling to, that is my stay, you know it Mother, as well as I. I want to touch Him, to hold Him as dearly as ever did that woman whose name I took, that time He was wandering over the plains of Galilee! I have told you all this a hundred times, and you have encouraged me, helped me. And then comes one who forbids me to speak endearing words to my Beloved—my Spouse—! I am too 'sensational' forsooth! Yes, that was the phrase he used. He says we must believe with the intellect not with the emotions, that within these walls we have let our emotions have too much play. And then he bids me consider the majesty or the justice of God. Words! Words! It is the love of Christ we desire! Intellect! It is a lie!"

"My dear, my dear! This is unseemly, compose yourself." And the Mother handed her a draught of water she had poured out, but Veronica refused the glass with a gesture.

The Prioress then slowly sat down, and there was silence, an electric unquiet silence, for a space. At last she spoke and her emotionless voice had the effect of eau de cologne sprinkled on the hot fevered head of a sick man tossing wearily to and fro, or of sweet air let into a fetid room.

"To look only at one truth to the exclusion of all others is no doubt a very grave, a very great and reprehensible mistake. In reading history, we generally, I think I might say without much fear of contradiction, invariably, find that heresy itself has sprung from an inordinate and impertinent insistence upon one point, which in time culminates in a distortion of all else and hence gross error. It is a case of perverted perspective. So Nestorians dwell overmuch on the divine nature of Our Lord; Sabellians on the unison of His nature with that of His Father; Taborites on biblical authority. And although, of course, these are extreme examples, yet their very exaggeration will serve to make clear what I mean. We also perhaps have our doubts and perplexities, our faults of belief, little and trifling indeed—God forbid it should ever be otherwise!—but we must be single, weaving, as it were, all colours duly into the tapestry of our Spiritual life, not taking up too much blue nor too much green, lovely as are the hues in themselves, lest we mar the divine pattern, which in its perfect harmony of all, is lovelier than any one."

She paused, as if collecting her thoughts, and the sister took advantage of the break to exclaim, "Ah! But some things—the love of Christ! It is impossible to exaggerate that!"

"Yet, Veronica, we must not forget the holiness and justice of God forever. Dwell upon, feed upon Divine Love as much as you will, but sometimes we must leaven it with the might and magnificence of the Most High. Blessed Torquemada and the sacred martyr Peter Arbues exemplified the wrath of God to a forward and disobedient generation!"

"All that means less than nothing to me—nothing at all! I don't think I am a bit afraid of God!"

"My child, do you feel no holy fear?"

"I often tremble with awe at the merest contemplation of the Divine. But it is the awe of love, no cringing and cowardice. Mother, I only want to love."

"Do you remember that Father Cassilis said in one of his sermons: There are other feasts in the year beside the Sacred Heart."

"Other feasts beside the Sacred Heart! I would be amply content if in the calendar there were only feasts of Jesus and Mary."

The two women instinctively from long habit bowed their heads at the two Holy Names.

"The other feasts, Veronica, add new lustre to Our Lady and Her Son. So when we mediate upon the Divine Omnipotence we do not belittle the love, we magnify it."

"Well, Mother, I will try to think of what you say. Only it is hard, very hard, to have to confess to a priest who is, you know it, antagonistic to one's whole idea and ideal."

"I allow it is hard, and I find it too. Yes, you must not suppose I am exempt from the worry of it all. When I was your age I was very like you, and I have experienced all you feel. Years have not blunted my spiritual emotions, they have only taught me to conceal them. Hard then when it seems very difficult, too difficult to be brave, I remember the pattern of the saints, of the dear great Saint," here the Prioress lowered her voice, which quivered with reverence and love, "Mother Teresa of Ávila. She was for years harassed by her confessors, by stupid priests and dull, all in ignorance working the heavenly will. Yet she never hesitated to obey them, and one day God sent her Juan de la Cruz. However, formerly, under obedience, she burned priceless pages wherein she had written her revelations, her visions, she, the one woman Doctor of the Church!"

"But I am no saint!"

"Try to be one, and in the attempt you will have succeeded."

"Mother, if you knew how my heart aches! The pain is almost physical."

"Indeed I am not sure that I ought not to restrict your fasts . . ."

Veronica raised her thin hands as if to ward off a blow. "Please, please . . ." she began.

"Do not be alarmed. I lay no commands upon you. I will not even advise you, for I should truly be very loath to interfere. Only if your state does not speedily improve we shall end by having you in the hands of Sister Infirmarian."

"When the soul is sick, Mother, how can the body but ail?"

"We must all hope for the best. I am, as you are fully aware, always ready and willing to discuss any spiritual difficulties and trials with you, and it is a sensible relief even to open one's sorrows. The mere recital of trouble often seems to assuage it, like the lancing of a boil. Live through the present by looking forward to the future, and perhaps ere very long God will send us a new director, one who will understand our method and our aims better than Father Cassilis. I have said as much as I can, if not rather more than I ought. You must respect my confidence. And now, child . . ."

Veronica rose at the finality of the tone, and without seeking to continue the conversation further, with a curtsey quitted the room.

VI

Even to an ordinary Catholic, to one who lives in mediocre mode, nor worse nor better than his fellows, to a man without any pretence of great spirituality, the choice of a suitable director is a thing of no light moment.

For in the recesses of the confessional, when, it may be, the church is dark and dim save for the lamp gleaming before the tabernacle shrouded in its silken curtains, save for a crude jet of naked gas turned low here and there in the sombre aisles, at this tense hour of mystery and shadow when each chapel seems an occult den of night, each tapestry may shroud some unthinkable secret in its folds, the penitent kneels and whispers through the little grating the true story of his soul, with its deformities, its sickness, the morbid thoughts, the passionate despair, its lusts and hybrid fantasies.

Within, the purple-stoled priest, unseen, himself unseeing the clammy brow beaded with dank drops, the frighted face, the writhing fingers, and only feeling hot nervous breath pant through the grill as the voice quivers and breaks in shame with the agony of the solitary sin, the incest, the aberration, sits vested with the tremendous authority of Almighty God, "et Deus" as some old pontiff of the triple crown once wrote, and anon when the last vice is sobbed out, the foulest abomination avowed, he puts the subtle question, he probes and balances the evil, weighing and rating spiritual filthiness.

He has studied in schools of strange literature: he has in his seminary perused the volumes of the Casuists, men who summoned up all that Moll, Krafft-Ebing and Tarnowsky have explained; who, standing aloof from it all, catalogue every vileness to which mankind is prone, every lubricity and refinement of lascivious fancy: he has the sage aphorisms of Emanuel Sa; the *Summary of Sins* by Stephen Bauny, whose master in metaphysics was the great Aristotle; the *Moral Theology* of Escobar, compiled from four and twenty doctors of divinity, a work which for authority has been compared to the mystic tome, sealed with seven seals, of the Apocalypse; in his hands are the writing of Diana the probabilist; the chapters of Sanchez and Tamburini upon reserved cases and upon marriage, wherein are discussed with the nicest impartiality and most equitably defined those chances, those flaws and spots, which exercise all the skill and acumen of medico-jurists today; he is a learner from Caramuel, than whom none has had a more absolute and profound knowledge of human nature, of all its sores and tender places, its infirmity and very pitifulness; from Debreyne pre-eminent in science and medicine; for him Bishop Bouveier wrote that pamphlet which is not disclosed without authorisation from the superior of the Diocesan seminary; for him Craisson, vicar general of Valence, compiled a scabrous treatise, *De rebus Veneris*, only placed in the hands of clerics under the strictest conditions; in fine to the director belongs the library of those theologians and professors, who, with inflexible psychiatry, do not hesitate as physicians of diseased minds to detail every infamy that brain can conceive or imagination supply, debating with nude frankness the most epicene and bestial conjunctions, only to be paralleled in the pagan pages of Elephantis and the impudicity of Aretine, scientifically expounding how and why this circumstance and that alter the nature of the sin.

Dangerous lore, but all necessary for him who sits and shrives, lest at some hour there come one who whispers a monstrous thing from which the confessor turns away in dread, and so a soul goes forth into the night.

Those little wooden boxes with their coarse stiff veils are the Gethsemane of many, but suddenly through the medium of His minister God, having taken the bleeding and sore soul and wrung it dry as one wrings a moist sponge, by a miracle of grace, heals, renews and washes it with balm in His own ineffable manner.

The cloaca is cleansed and made pure.

And if for the ordinary individual, for offices of cleansing and cure, which become almost mechanical, a skilled confessor, a priest of tact, of knowledge, is so necessary, how much more is he not essential in the direction of those who aim at a greater perfection? When the processes of purification are past, the personality comes forth to meet personality, to master and to guide. Vast are the responsibilities, and if he fail to get into sympathy with the soul he seeks to lead, then must the arcane sacrament oftimes be not only nugatory and vain, but torpid and stagnant, even immediately noxious.

In the direction of a nun, of a life almost wholly lived on the spiritual plane, seeing that she has put away the world, that it has dissolved from about her as a vapour and a dream, the intervention of a ghostly counsellor, however pious, however learned and devout, who is not an innate occultist, an abider in the secret sanctuary, could not be aught but impious in the highest degree.

Contemplatives should be governed by mystics, and in all the records of visionaries and ecstatics, there are few cries more bitter, few pages more sodden with human tears than those wherein they tell how they were misunderstood and trammelled by the very tutelage set to encourage and enlarge.

The Mercedarians were in the position of finding themselves completely severed from their director. Much to the secular, to the religious such a state meant the gradual abruption of all. For the chaplain is to a large extent the centre of convent life. He has it in his power, if not directly at least indirectly and quite as effectively, to regulate devotions exterior to the rule, to abridge and circumcise.

In practice these things are the provinces of the Prioress, yet in a case where a director chose to assert and stretch his authority without openly clashing with the Supervisor he can alter much and even draw the vitality of much more away, hushing it, so that the complexion of the inner life is changed, and he moulds the house to his will and liking.

VII

Following the ancient Spanish custom, the nuns, upon all feasts of the Virgin, used blue vestments for the Mass. They had many sets, splendid and antique, brought from cities of the south, dalmaticas for boy thurifers, garments redolent almost yet with the fumes of censors swung by olive-tinted lads, gracious and

Greek, in the choir of cathedrals long ago: stoles, their shoulders heavy with silver broidery; great azure velvet capes, upon whose orphreys appeared symbols of transcendental meaning, the Ivory Tower, the Garden Enclosed, the Bundle of Myrrh that lay all night betwixt the breasts of the Beloved, the Perfumed Rose, worked in silks and gay spooled thread by some amorous Carmen or Dolores behind the latticed window of Andalusia and Cadiz.

Generally the colour blue has been proscribed, and the holy days of Mary must put aside the hue of God's sky and ocean to love themselves in the normal white or gold, for which very reason the convent clung dearly to its peculiar use, and loved to watch the solemn priest walk with downcast eyes from the sacristy whilst the hieratic chasuble of larkspur or celestine hung down stiff and stately around, to see, as he turned his back ascending with clasped hands and murmured prayer to the altar, the jewelled medallion of their Queen, encrusted with diamonds, pearls and pale sapphire stones.

It was the morning of the feast of the Virgin de Bonaria, the Star of the Sea, whose image had been so wonderfully brought to the lone shrine of Cagliani, where the waves break sullenly at the base of stern Sardinian cliffs, and Sister Elisabeth was busy setting out the liturgical vestments.

She drew from the shelf, sweetly smelling of lavender and cedar dust, the chasuble of pale blue satin, pillared with costly silver, pictured with the Immaculate Conception, and spread it upon the broad table above, which was discreetly covered with a clean linen cloth lest any fleck mar or dirt the costly vestments.

Next she laid out the maniple, crosswise, and deftly arranged the stole so that it traced the sacred letter, initials of the adorable name, Mary.

Above this was set the girdle, the fine alb with its skirt of rose lace spread over black satin, the long-stringed amice, that in vesting the celebrant should find each in their turn ready to his hand.

The server had adjusted the markers in the missal and was lighting the candles, when Father Cassilis entered.

Without delay, he twisted himself out of cloak and hat, and began to wash his hands at the basin, muttering the prescribed prayer, "Da, Domine, Virtutem manibus meis . . ."

Sister Elisabeth entered the choir, and took her place.

A few moments passed. Her preparatory devotions ended, she waited for the entrance of the priest, turning the pages of her book and letting her eye catch a phrase here and there.

The tapers burned very wan and yellow in the sunlight, flickering a little from invisible draught.

The altar waited the advent of the celebrant.

It seemed very long before he came that morning,

Several minutes had gone and the sacristy door yet remained closed. The nuns began to look at each other in surprise, until at last the Prioress raised her head, and Sister Elisabeth reading both inquiry and permission in her face, with a genuflection hurried out to see what was amiss.

Father Cassilis stood in the act of donning a chasuble of white brocade. The blue vestments had been pushed aside and this set, plain and very simple, selected in their stead.

As the door quivered he looked up and seeing the astonished nun began in a low but peremptory voice: "Sister, the rubric dictates white. What can I do with all these obsolete garments, these blue chasubles of yours? Why too such rich vestments, pray, for this commemoration of Our Lady, a memorial that however excellent in the first place, is fast becoming fantastic by reason of the lying legends that have grown up like fungi about the truth? No more of your fancy colours for me, if you please."

He signed to the acolyte to precede him, took up the chalice, and with a reverence to the cross passed into the chapel, leaving the Sister half in anger, half in tears, wholly thunderstruck and wondering if the stars were not going to fall.

VIII

In the privacy of her cell she knelt, wrapt in contemplation.

The rule prescribed set hours of meditation for the community in chapel, but over and beyond these every nun, according to the spirit of the Order even if the written letter did not absolutely direct the when and where, was bound each day to pass many another hour besides in that mystic contemplation which leads to supreme union with the supernatural.

The garden, among whose walks and lawns she had been wont to spend so much of her time, now distorted her imagination. It was full of scent and colour and life, things which seemed to her in some psychic way to interfere with the vocation to which she was called, to elongate Christ from her,

Surely that was the end and aim of her existence, she thought, to arrive at an embrace with Christ, which should be dearer and nearer than any earthly symbol or marital copulation. As she advanced, nothing must be allowed to hinder, nothing must come between. Some days, at some moments, He stood hard by, she had only to have reached out her hand to have touched Him, but of late He had receded and was deaf to her calling.

This seemed very sad to her.

With outstretched arms she knelt before the bare wall to which was affixed a large crucifix, gaunt and realistic.

Once, reading of Buddhist monks and Indian fakirs, of the gymnosophists, who meditate in a state of complete inanimation, a coma brought about by gazing upon vacancy, she had attempted to pray with her eyes staring immovably at the blank white-washed wall of a corridor, but had only succeeded in giving herself a monstrous migraine, in spite of which she did not move even to unclasp her hands when a fly walked over the fingers, remembering how at Paray-le-Monial the Vision had rebuked the blessed Ecstatica Margaret Mary for uncrossing her left foot from over her right when she was cramped and numb from the one posture.

She was very hungry that afternoon, for she had refused all food in the refectory and it was long ere the next meal.

She felt a little giddy too, and as her brows involuntarily contracted the lids drooped wearily.

***

"Come, O My chosen one, and I will establish my throne with Thee, for the King hath greatly desired Thy beauty"

The Divine Desire, that was the subject of meditation.

She thought how in Canticles, the epithalamium of Divine Love, the Bridegroom had come and put His hand in at the door.

The spouse, she was some henna-eyed houri, whose glances were provocative behind the snowy folds of her burnous. An odalisque clad in scarlet and green, full-bosomed, almost melancholy, as the Easterners love.

All the long summer day she had laid upon her divan, heaped with soft cushions, in the shade of the harem. From under her heavy painted lashes she watched the white doves with their coral feet strutting about the court, cooing to each other, amorously rubbing their beaks in gentle caresses, and the dusky girl burned and languished for her lover. Her olive-tinted cheeks paled beneath the maquillage, and she shivered a little.

The day grew hotter, pregnant with noon, and the splash of cool water was pleasant to the ear.

Her slaves came forth bearing fragrant coffee, rich and black, sweetmeats and comfits drenched with attar of roses, sherbet, in wide open bowls. Eunuchs fanned her and sprinkled the place with perfumes, whose very breath was voluptuous, full of dreams, whilst some ancient negress tied her luxuriant tresses and whispered tales of her own native land, a sun-parched track of arid plain, where swarthy men hate and love in fierce animal fashion.

Yet the day seemed overlong. But at last when the sky grew violet and stars rushed out in glittering companies, she rose and she walked undulatingly, the bangles tinkled upon her ankle like the chime of camel-bells over the desert.

They spread the couch with rugs of Damascus and Kurdistan, with thrice-dipped coverlets from Tyrian looms; they burned joss sticks in brazen vessels, frank-incense in silver thuribles, and the chamber was odorous with the sweet savour.

They undressed her, and wrapped her lithe limbs in garments of meshy silk, gauzes whose transparency was stitched with argent threads, diapered with vermilion flowers; tussares woven delicately by little almond-eyed men of orange complexion in far Japan and the cities of Cathay; robes all sewn with gems, which, when she moves, burn into flame of a thousand colours, as though there had swarmed there a vast multitude of insects and golden beetles, whose shiny wings were iridescent with fire and beauty, glittering jade-green, phosphorescent with rose and almandine, ochre, lapis lazuli and speckled pyrites. The bracelets of rough red metal weighed down her wrists, barbaric charms and amulets glinted among the curling of her hair.

Strange perfumes were scattered from antique pomanders of Persia and Kabool, the air was dense with neroli, coreopsis, jasmine, musk and maréchale, outside the lattices the giant magnolia blossoms exhaled their impure chastity, fatiguing the night with the exotic languor of their caresses.

They lit lamps of luscious oil and set upon the carven tables of sandalwood, upon stool of ebony inlaid with nacre, cakes, fruit, sugared marchpane, flasks of wine, yellow and red; more potent draughts were in curious bottles sealed with the signet of the merchant, opium, satyrion, bhang, aphrodisiacs and narcotics.

She lay upon the couch beneath the Oriental night, and an operatic moon watched her, as she swooned with fervent expectance of coming love, and her crimsoned lips, red as a fierce anthurium, shone fuller and moister, parting for the avid kiss.

Then the door opened and the hand of the Bridegroom lifted the latch: He stood in shadow upon the groundsel.

But her heart knew that it was He ere her eyes saw, and the born appassionata ran to meet Him, to draw Him into the chamber prepared and the bed was made ready.

Surely the joy of that moment which, as S. John of the Cross says, unites the Lover and the Beloved, when, amid the lilies forgotten she is changed into her Love, far outweighs the weariness of waiting hours, the day-long vigil, the sick and aching tedium until it was a void in the breast, the temples throbbed, and food became loathly to the taste.

Bride of Christ, what nuptials are yours!

All the expectation, all the hopes and yearning fears, all the kisses and consummation of love that fond girls dream of on their maiden couches, blushing daintily even in sleep to image the caresses of an earthly husband, are knit up and concentrated and thrice redoubled with a surpassing energy of desire and divine vehemence in the spousals of those virgins who, as the ancient responsory of the mystic Carmelites sings, loving Christ are ever chaste, are received in His embrace and remain yet pure and undefiled.

Could we but catch a spark of the fervours of those Saints who walked with God indeed! At midnight in the church of San Domenico a nun paces up and down the long shadowy aisles, but not alone! For with Catherine walked the visible form of her Bridegroom, the Christ. He comforts her, and stays her with words of ineffable love. His wounded hands hold those of His stigmatised bride, she who shared so joyously in the Passion of her Spouse. And so at her voice, nay, only looking upon her, hearts were changed.

Gaily goes the Franciscan Tertiary over the Umbrian hills amid the purpling vineyards, wrapped in the embrace of Him who shed His Blood for her. She trembles with delight as she hears her lover whispering "I love thee more than any woman in the vale of Spoleto."

Being in prayer, the Seraphic Mother Teresa, wan and faint with almost continuous rapture, her heart transfixed with a fiery dart, her soul tearing itself to pieces within her, suddenly beholds the Sacred Hands of excessive beauty, and then as she swoons in hysteria of too intolerable felicity the Divine Face looks into hers. And finally upon the feast of S. Paul at mass she sees the radiance of the whole Sacred Humanity.

The wounded frame of Lucia de Narni; a daughter of Dominic, although her pure flesh was emaciated and scarred, starven with abstinences and fasts, exhaled sweetest fragrancy as becomes those delicious lilies blooming in the terrestrial gardens of God. Satiate and languishing with ecstasies she would cry aloud that her very vitals were convulsed within her, her body a holocaust of passion. And so during the offering of the Sacrifice she saw upon the altar the Babe of Bethlehem who gazed upon her with eyes desirous, radiant with love, eyes that shone as the stars upon a clear frosty night. And anon He nested in her virgin bosom.

In a remote convent of the Visitation, a humble nun, the fairest flower in the garden of S. Francis de Sales, watched before the tabernacle in weariness and despondency; the Saviour stood before her and opened the inexhaustible treasures of the Sacred Heart wounded and bloody with love for man, showing her that Heart to be a very living flame.

What hallowed nuptials of mystery were these! Ah, Virgin brides it may be that amidst your trances and deliria the Divine Love proved so human after all!

In the city of Lima dwelt Rose, who at first was called Isabel. Enflamed with continual prayer, whilst of most tender age, solemnly she affianced herself to Christ.

Such was her tender beauty that the young men, the Peruvians, desired her, and seeing the comeliness of her eyes, uplifted, it may be, at mass to gaze upon the white wafer, which was her secret spouse, they sought her hand in marriage, but she refused them all.

For, one morning, as she walked in her little garden, a flight of butterflies, sulphur-yellow, pink, blue, purple emperors, red admirals, peacock moths, moths with great velvet wings dusk as a funereal pall, circled about her head, but one alone, and his wings were black and white, settled softly upon her hair, which thing she took to be a symbol and a sign that she was to don the habit of Dominic.

This she did, "at an age," wrote Dubonnet, "when girls are for the most part well confirmed in all the hateful practices of coquetry, and attend with gusto, rather than with distaste, the hideous desires and terrible satisfactions of men." And when she had vowed herself wholly to Christ, her beauty increased until it became almost divine, a celestial gift. For her Spouse delighted to adorn His flower. To men it often seemed as though her features were iridescent, and her eyes shone like candles.

She was indeed a Rose, which filled the New World with the fragrance of its perfumes, a flower to be plucked but by the pierced Hand of the Master, and unto this day the Friar Preachers amid their ancient liturgy pray humbly that we also may run in the odour of her sweetness.

Delicate and exquisite of soul, Aubrey Beardsley loved her well, and wrote of her in his rococo fantasy

Under the Hill, and pictured her for us, beautifully, in the "Assumption of S. Rose," where we see Madonna, very Spanish in her cape and crown, embracing the Peruvian virgin, who, having crimsoned her lips and painted her face, came out to pray in the oratory of Mary Immaculate.

For perchance as Mary looked upon the maid who loved Her Son, she remembered the home of Nazareth and that springtime when She Herself had been a bride in a Spousal more mysterious and ecstatic than any since the world began or shall be.

Osanna Andreasi was only six years old, when, as she walked one noon along the banks of the Mantuan Po she fell into a trance, and saw a seraph who took her by the hand and led her into the chapel of the Nine Choirs where in some mysterious evocation she beheld the fundamental constituents and the elements of creation praising and loving the Eternal God.

Which spectacle so deeply touched her that she prayed most insistently to be shown the perfect way of love. After much perseverance there appeared an infant, very comely, more radiant than the Sun, whiter than snow, full of charm and grace, exhaling the air of heaven. "His eyes," she writes, "were lovely beyond compare; He fixed them upon me full of love, which drew my very soul from me, and as I contemplated Him I was ravished. Whereupon His countenance changed and He became of larger stature, crowned with thorns, charged with a cross, and in a voice of perfect melody He said: 'My love, O my well-beloved, I am the Son of the Virgin Mary, of Mine Own wish and will do I take virgins to be My spouses, and wedding them their maidenhood is preserved.'" Osanna replied, "I love Thee with my whole heart!" and from that hour the Divine Bridegroom was united so closely to her that her life seemed one long delirium of love.

To how many thousands more has the Spouse come, how many thousand thousand has He not merged in the infinite shoreless ocean of His desire!

Every Order has its scores of Saints and Beati, the visionaries and ecstaticas, every town and village swells their number.

Whole convents, not merely solitary individuals, have been inundated with love and become schools of the highest mysticism. Elisabeth Steiglin, the correspondent of Suso, wrote the lives of many sisters of the house of Thöss, all of whom were perpetually illuminated. The convent of Schönensteinbach was the theatre of esoteric phenomena. Among the Beguines mystics abounded. Here was experienced the extraordinary kiss of Jesus, when the nuns at their communion tasted a savour sweeter than honey, which when the host was placed between their lips, inundated their senses.

The communion! What a joy that had once been to Veronica, when with her tongue she might touch the very flesh of her Beloved. There was a rumour among the nuns that Sister Juliana had once verily seen the Divine Flesh palpitating and living in the host, and Veronica made it her daily prayer that for her also the veil might be one moment withdrawn.

She hankered after objective experiences, and read with delight how that one morning when S. Teresa had received the host from the hand of S. Juan, her mouth was filled with blood which ran out all over her dress.

That day Veronica had not allowed a crumb of food, nor a drop of water to pass her lips, nothing but the wafer of the Eucharist, and yet after all these hours of fasting and struggle her mouth remained dry, her palate was parched and burning. Would she never attain to those raptures, for which her soul lusted! As the thought of disappointment, of a positive failure, entered her mind, she shuddered from head to foot.

"Osculetur me osculo oris sui!" O that he would kiss me with the lips of his mouth!

The cry of the Shulamite was Veronica's also.

A kiss, for the kiss is the birth of love. Where lips have never touched it is hard for souls to meet. The kiss of his mouth. No empty, formal salute but a deep passionate clinging of lips to lips, a mingling of that breath which is in some way the symbol of life itself. And when one considers the beauty of the mouth, often more expressive than eyes or even hands, it seems exquisitely fitting that thence should spring the knowledge of passion and desire.

She thought of the handsome contadini of Naples and the Parthenopean coast, lads with full curving lips red as the core of a pomegranate in the nut-brown of their smooth oval faces. Where the air is fragrant with oleander and rosemary, with the perfume of orange blossoms before the round gold fruit gleams through the dark green leafery, where purple cataracts of wisteria pour over loggia and house-wall, whilst banksia, scarlet, yellow or white, runs riot among the hedges and clamours the wild olive trunks and pines, when at nightfall the moon, like a divine alchemist, melts Sacramento's bay into purest silver, nature herself is the teacher of her children, and her first lesson is that of love. Soon they know the secret of love's mystery, the kiss. And their kisses are as those which Martial sang when Diadumenus was kind, sweeter than the apple bitten by the pearly teeth of some gentle girl, than the pale flame which licks up Saracen incense, than amber chaffed in the hand, than a rose garland crowning hair drenched in odorous essences.

She thought of Guenevere, and how the Round Table perished and Arthur, tended by weeping queens, passed to the Vale of Avilion, and all because:

> "In that garden fair
> Came Lancelot walking; this is true, the
>   kiss,
> Wherewith we kissed in meeting that
>   spring day,
> I scarce dare talk of the remembered lips."

So sweet was their sin that, centuries after, reading the old romance Francesca da Rimini allowed her lips to be touched by Paolo, and for the fruit of that kiss, was doomed to be carried eternally through the swirl and night of the Second Circle; yet was Dante deceived, for if she was with her lover she could not have been in Hell.

Again the nun thought of Maurice Greiffenhagen's picture *An Idyll*, as she had once seen it in some Liverpool gallery.

The sun dips beyond the far horizon, a lurid ball crouching to rest behind the shadow trees. The flame of scarlet poppies and pale moon daisies are rife in the long lush meadow grass. The tall black-haired girl has fallen into the arms of her lover, at a moment of utter lassitude, the last abandonment. Her long arms droop idly to her side, she is too languid to divine them about his neck: she does not resist, she does not insist, docile, passive: but absolute surrender is painted on her face, and her lips sigh apart with the foreknowledge of love's extreme ecstasy. The shepherd has come to her over the fields, and clasped her in his stalwart embrace, pressing her close, body to body. His face is in shade as his mouth crushes on her cheek. As they stand together thus, strangely noticeable is the bronze of his naked limbs, loosely girt with a sheepskin, in contrast to her white shoulders and bosom whence slips the veiling of mauve.

She remembered how striking the picture had seemed to her in its realisation of desire. And as she looked at it her companion had pressed her hand significantly. The young American, with whom she had lingered those few days after landing from New York! He had accompanied her to London. She remembered how he had paid bridge debts and lavished gifts upon her; for he was very much in love and quite rich enough to afford it. He had even pressed her to marry him, but she refused. She liked him too much for that.

She wondered what excuse she had made him at the time, why exactly she refused. Was the motive pure unselfishness, goodness in fact? She knew how they had separated after deliberately drifting apart, for she was getting too fond of him. One afternoon when she thought he had left England, was ever gone out of her life, he had practically forced his way into her boudoir, and there burst into a passionate declaration of love, falling upon his knees.

Would she ever forget him as he knelt in the amber lamp-light, his upturned face white and drawn with emotion, and the fire flickered in the silver toys and china teacups?

". . . I love you, Olivia . . . oh, I swear I love you . . ."

And she had forced herself to laugh at his "acting," to treat him as a silly trifling boy, but her heart hurt her, and he had left the room a man.

His fingers had clutched at her dress, but she swished it away petulantly, almost disdainfully. It was a princess robe of rose pink silk covered with a foam of Venetian point. How her rings, the diamonds, had glistened with the quick movement of her hand!

The swift shadow of a bird on the wing fell across her through the little grated window high up in the wall.

Outside a sparrow chirruped loudly.

She opened her eyes and experienced something like a shock of horror when they fell on the folds of her habit, white; snowy white as a fold of lace.

She almost saw hands, phantom, bodiless hands, writhing and striving to catch her scapula or the hem of her skirt.

With a gasp she raised her head and there met her gaze the Face of the Crucified looking down at her from the Cross, sadly, reproachfully, in weariness.

IX

Under the dome, in the centre of an almost circular apse, stood the high altar raised on a flight of seven steps. On either side were ranged the stalls of the nuns, two semi-circles in double rows. The seats, of dark oak rich with heavy carving and somewhat florid ornamentation, were copied from some cathedral of Southern Spain. The whole floor was composed of inlaid wood, cinnamon, pear, walnut and mahogany.

A heavy rood-screen, so solid and impenetrable, that it amply served the purpose of a grille, divided the nuns' choir from the public portion, which latter was small hardly a quarter of the whole building, and but scantily furnished with a few rush-bottomed chairs. At time of office and mass a heavy veil was drawn across the screen from within, so that the figures beyond were absolutely invisible, and the very voices seemed to come from afar.

The vault and cupola were painted with a fresco portraying the Translation of the Holy House of Loreto, wafted through the air in glory, surrounded by mystic forms of cherubim and archangels.

The marbles of which the altar itself was composed were of the most exquisite kind, all wrought with countless designs of fruit, flowers, vases, birds, scrolls, garlands, enriched with red carnelian, agate, rock crystal, topaz, orichale, onyx, jasper, and other precious material.

High in the centre, supported by bronze amorini and seraph heads, was a picture, Mary, the Mother of Mercy, crowned with a golden coronet that glittered with gems. On either side in the lateral niches of green Campan stood statues, the one to the right, S. Maria de Cervellon, the first Mercedarian nun, the one to the left, the Spanish beata, Marianna di Gesù.

The mensa, upheld by basalt columns, was of porphyry, but the body of the altar was hollow, a shrine, closed in front by a sheet of plate glass, that reflected in its crystal depths the flicker of the sanctuary lamp which swung before it.

Herein lay the relics of S. Chrysocomus, a Roman lad, who preferred chastity and death by the centurion's sword to rivalry with Sporus in Nero's embraces. As is customary the bones had been embedded in a wax figure; modelled by a celebrated artist of Seville.

Lying rather in sleep, so it seemed, than in death, the martyr was represented as a stripling, some sixteen years old, beautiful with all the freshness of immortal youth. Upon his smooth cheeks flushed the bloom of a boyhood which could never know change nor decay, his limbs were moulded with an almost feminine delicacy and comeliness. His head rested upon a cushion of white satin tasselled with gold: the long fair hair hung down over the white shoulders. The face was slightly turned to one side, so prettily, so graceful, that in the dim light which filtered fitfully through the sapphire, green and crimson of the chapel windows, the gazer might well imagine he saw the long silken lashes quiver, the bosom respire with life.

A scarlet tunic, loosely girt about the hips with a golden girdle, fell from his breasts to his slender thighs, leaving the arms and legs bare. His feet were fitted with sandals of Cordova leather, studded with jewelled knobs and nails.

Across his neck could be seen the deep gash of the steel, but it was a dainty wound, for all its realism not over obtrusive, and the drops that had fallen on the white skin seemed more like petals of geranium than blood from a death blow.

Between his feet lay the little vase from the catacombs, which contained a sponge soaked with his blood, and one hand clasped a silver palm of exquisite workmanship.

Reposing there he seemed like some pagan deity or demigod, some fair Grecian boy, in the midst of this chapel buried in honour and worship of a great sorrow, to plead a death of agony and shame.

Was it Hymenaeus, beloved of the Evening Star, or Hyacinth, or Cyparissus, the favourite of Pan, or Endymion, whom Hypnos, god of slumber, sent to sleep with open eyes in order that he might always gaze upon their beauty?

Ganymede, tending the sheep among the vales of Ida when the eagle sped from heaven like a radiant comet rushing through the eastern sky and falling among the woods of Troy, was not more comely; nor Hylas whom the nymphs of the haunted mere caught in their white arms and held love's prisoner. Graceful, voluptuous even, so might Adonis have looked when he fell, his flank scared by the boar, whilst fond Cytherea beat her breast in vain.

Grifonetto, "un altro Ganimede," lying covered with dagger thrusts upon the flags of that piazza where the Perugian Duomo, forlorn and desolate, yet looks down upon Pisano's fountain, so beautiful that as he gasps out his life there, Atalanta his mother, her dress dabbled in his steaming blood, kneels over him and blesses him, although the day before had driven him from her presence and cursed him bitterly, so comely that the dry old chronicler breaks out into rapturous praise of Hellenic loveliness, was not more fair than the boy Saint who lay beneath the Mercedarian altar.

Many a nun had loved him spiritually, and for his sake the hours she spent in the church before his shrine became more perfervid, her devotion intenser.

Many a nun had wandered with him in the land of dreams walking by his side as he held her with sweet words of passion and caress, even sinning it might be, but the grass was green beneath their feet, the sky was blue and open overhead, the air sweet and fragrant with springtide, the bushes dappled pink and white with hawthorn, primroses and daffodils yellow in the fields, life was young and gay; but all wakened to a stern round of penitence and prayer: the grey chills of winter dawn and icy frost duly dispelled the warm sunshine of fairy isles.

※

The chapel was the heart of the convent. Here the nuns assembled many times a day for office and meditation.

At midnight, whether in summer when sleep had been impossible for stifling atmosphere and lack of air, when irritating prickles of heat would run up and down the skin, itching torture as the fevered head tossed wearily upon the flock pillow and both habit and blanket grew stiff and dank with sweat, whether in January when the cells, fireless, cheerless, were dark and arctic cold, for outside the soft snow was falling noiselessly like wool and frost traced fantastic patterns upon the dull glazing of the high barred windows, whilst the water in each tiny ewer congealed to ice, the breath hung like smoke, fingers were numb and blue, these weak women, coffined behind wall and grate, awoke when the world slept, and aching with weariness or pain, faint from vigil and scourge, chanted the solemn office of matins and lauds, hours long with the ninefold lections and grave psalmody.

The night liturgies were at once severe penance and exultant joy. For then it seemed that the endless work of expiation had reached the acme of its round, and although the body was tired beyond measure, the soul reached more boldly toward the invisible.

Outside in the world when all seems most still, red sin is walking abroad with dainty tread thro' palace and hovel, going delicately in perfumed pomp of beauty and pride. Man has bought him the wares chaffered in lust's mart, the pavement of great cities. The world slumbers or but wakes to fulfil the whispers of bright-eyed desire, some in clambering, some in drunkenness.

And at those very moments when their sisters, sold upon the highways and squares, lie in the arms of the purchaser who esteems them less than the price he pays, tires of them in the first bought kiss, the nuns wake in their cold virginity to assail highest heaven with their intercessions, calling, but vainly, upon the world to arise and sing unto the Lord, to rejoice in God our salvation.

X

"Yes, it is quite true, Reverend Mother, but I cannot imagine how it got known. I never can imagine how things do get known in this house."

"Well, Mother Aña, I hardly feel at liberty to tell you who brought it under my notice, but it was quite indelicately done.'

"Yes . . . yes. I am sure I have not spoken of it to anyone."

"Nobody could accuse you of being so indiscreet: yet perhaps by your manner you gave some indication of disliking Father Cassilis."

"Disliking, Reverend Mother? I admit it, but how can one control these emotions? It is impossible." The nun crossed and uncrossed her hands, murmuring querulously.

"At least we should try to veil them, should we not?"

"Sometimes they are too violent for us. I have never broached the subject myself, but now you speak to me of it, I have not the slightest hesitation in telling you frankly that Father Cassilis is exercising, what is to my mind, a most deteriorating influence on us all!" Then with a sudden burst of heat: "Pos Dios crucificado! The man would change our prayers, our ideals, and lay his fingers on the holy rule itself if he darest. I have no patience with these islanders. They have the heretic in their marrow." And the old Spanish woman signed herself with an opulent cross.

"I never realised how strongly you felt on the point. Of course I knew that he was very far from satisfying us and did much that was contrary to our practice, but until a day or two since I had no idea of the general friction and unhappiness."

"Look at Veronica, Mother. What better example could you want than she is? Her very face is a picture of distress—spiritual, mind you, not bodily."

"Yes, I know, Mother Aña, I know. It is dreadful. But I am so loth to initiate anything of this kind. One never can tell where it will lead. Quarrels with our chaplain, the Archbishop dissatisfied and worried when he has so much to occupy his time. Monsignor Keppel is only just returned home and to annoy him with a grievance unless of necessity would be unfair. I had thought to defer all this unpleasant business until he came to profess Sister Celestine, but really now . . ." and the Prioress sighed sadly.

"Ay, Mother, no time must be lost. It is difficult but we cannot go on as we are!"

"So it seems," and she passed her hand over her forehead with that gesture of utter lassitude old age brings to the weary.

"Alma mia," cried Mother Aña in a tenderer tone, leaning forward and laying her hand upon the trembling hand of her friend, "it is necessary . . . believe me, else I would not trouble you thus, you who have so much to bear, our complaints, our troubles, our shortcomings of every day, and I know you shrink from interfering, for we are only strangers you and I, after all, not of these English, no. But needs must, this priest is revolutionising the whole house. He must go."

"Indeed, if it must be I will take the matter in hand. Veronica was with me not a week since begging me to move, and I could give the poor girl no satisfaction but patience. Yet now I find you all wish it, and it is apparent you do, I will write to Monsignor without delay."

"Sister Juliana feels it most acutely. Oh, no!" in answer to a gesture of the Prioress, "she has not spoken, any more than I."

"I will write tomorrow morning."

"It is high time" rejoined Mother Aña relapsing to her former peevishness, and then turning to the third nun she cried. "And you Mother Werburgh, what do you think?"

The Novice Mistress, who had been sitting with folded hands mechanically slipping the ivory beads through her fingers and gazing somewhat vacantly out of the French window opposite, seemed to wake from a profoundly pious meditation.

Thus suddenly appealed to she started for a moment as though she had not quite followed the conversation.

"I agree to everything Revered Mother may suggest," she replied.

"Quite so, but we want your own opinion upon the subject of discussion. Don't you think with me that the Archbishop ought to be asked to remove Father Cassilis?"

"Why, certainly, certainly, Mother Aña. I understood we had determined all that long ago. He has upset my whole novitiate. I find my children full of perplexities and doubts. The other day Ursula was in tears after her confession."

"But why did you not tell me this before, Mother Wenburgh?" asked the Prioress obviously disturbed.

"Well, Mother, your bronchitis has pulled you down and I would not worry you until you are completely recovered and strong enough to cope with these difficulties."

"So we all felt," added Mother Aña.

"Moreover," continued the Novice Mistress, "I have always taken it that Father Cassilis is only a temporary chaplain, and I have counteracted anything that seemed to me amiss or unsuitable in his teaching by my instructions."

"I am relieved to hear it."

"Undoubtedly only one things remains, to make a change. And, Mother, would it not be better to ask for a regular as chaplain? These parish priests do not or cannot understand us."

"Yes, I will press that point."

"We are amply rich enough to afford it."

"Now that we have spoken so freely," said Mother Aña in a lower tone, "has it never struck you that Father Cassilis in his sermons ventures upon, if not heretical, at least dangerous opinions?"

The three nuns glanced at each other apprehensively.

"So you have noticed it too," murmured the Novice Mistress in an equally subdued voice.

"Yes, it seemed to me he is only saved by vagueness from heresy."

"Oh, Mother, do you really think . . . ?"

The old nun nodded her head with pursed lips in a quick incisive manner.

"But I cannot say I ever remarked anything of the kind!" expostulated the Prioress.

"Oh, I am right I am sure. Mark my words the man is a traitor, a Modernist." She hissed the latter name with all the contempt and loathing of which her foreign nature was capable and her old eyes blazed with flame.

Mother Wenburgh with difficulty stifled a scream.

"Dios! It is possible!" ejaculated the Prioress blanching with horror.

For reply the nun was content to nod her head, not perhaps altogether unpleased at the effect she had created.

"That is enough. I write tonight!" And she rose to her feet.

"I am grieved at this. Sorely grieved, but I do not see how it could have happened otherwise under the circumstances," said Aña, who lingered a moment, to the Mother softly. "Ay to close my eyes in our own country, to see Burgos, or my Seville,

> Sevilla del alma mia!
> Sevilla de mi consuelo!
> Quien estuviera en Sevilla
> Aunque durmiera en e suelo!"

Their eyes filled with tears.

XI

It was not the ordinary parlour of a presbytery, but a workroom, the study of a busy man.

As he sat by the window the light of the afternoon sun clearly showed his clear-cut intellectual face, hard and stern for all its acumen, yet now contracted with deep and serious thought. The open letter in his hand, closely written sheets of flimsy foreign paper, gave clue to his abstraction.

At his elbow upon the little oval table stood his tea untasted. He had obviously poured it out before opening his correspondence, intending to sip as he read, and now it was growing cold and sloppy. The spoon remained in the cup, just as he had left stirring.

The bread and butter, four thick slices, was untasted; the home-made cake uncut.

He gazed out of the window sadly. It was come, the blow which although he had hardly expected he had realised as an overhanging possibility. Yes, he had never blinded himself: his was a dangerous work, a course apt to be maligned, misrepresented, but nevertheless in the service of truth and enlightenment he dared all.

For surely men's minds must be more open, it only wanted pioneers to cleanse the dust of centuries, to make belief freer, better, wider in every sense of the word. However, it had fallen. Well, there must be no drawing back. Indeed was it not too late even if he wished? Had there not been danger signals all along the line?

Four years ago, abruptly and without explanation, he had been removed from the chair of exegetics at Calcott and sent to Osney, a hamlet where the mission was a mere handful, services held in an ill-disguised barn.

To say mass, to catechise, to counsel and confess a score of rustics, these duties had allowed him ample time for study. And at hand lay Oxford with the Bodleian, its colleges, Balliol, home of modern philosophies; a new generation of dons.

There had been great opportunities. He remembered that Friday afternoon when Sabatier publically lectured at Manchester College on "les grandes Questions Religieuses, Autorité de l'Église, de la Bible . . ." How eloquently the Frenchman spoke . . . ! More he had been able to spend whole mornings in research. The months at Osney were by no means wasted, for it was there that the material accumulated for his last book. And he had been happy . . . happy in a way it might be . . . but sensibly neglected. He had never occupied the pulpit at S. Aloysius, beloved of Christian undergraduates; the Cowley Capuchins and Sisters of Begbroke ignored his existence.

He had been disappointed in his success. No doubt *The Gospel and the New Law* made some stir at the time, but then it was published while he was still at Calcott, and he looked for a wide discussion to follow *Catholic Expansion*, which had seemingly fallen almost sterile to the ground with imperceptible results. Yet the first had been a tour de force, little more, and the last comprised the epitome of many months study, correspondence, and thought.

Suddenly he was appointed chaplain to this Mercedarian convent. He let his mind dwell on them rather bitterly, with self-admitted annoyance. The whole house was foreign to the core, foreign in thought, in aim, in every detail of life. It was hard for a philosophic mind,—no doubt his mind was philosophic, analytically so,—to be brought to bear upon the doings of these nuns who seemed to move in a world of poetry and hysteria. Mysticism had no use for him, the rustics were preferable to these. At Osney he had at least had plenty of time on his hands, and was undisturbed. Here a thousand irritations beset his path daily.

He bit his lips sharply . . . At any rate, now he would hardly be suffered to remain on. That was if things took their course, which they must. Submission and retraction, an absolute surrender of principle, in fact, were the methods some might adopt in his situation. But he was determined to hold his own, to show himself bold without arrogance, staunch without obstinacy. He glanced down at the open letter. The torn envelope that lay on the floor was stamped with the Roman postmark.

". . . cannot be astonished. You must be aware how suspiciously *The Gospel and the New Law* was received here. The Italian translation is tacitly forbidden. I am only surprised that the storm has not bust sooner . . . . . . This volume has, I have it on good authority, been handed to the Holy Father himself . . . . a book denounced by three so powerful adversaries must be condemned. You write you do not know who they may be. Are you jesting? It is no secret here—First there is the Bishop of Laurium. The others are regulars. Don Kenyon the Benedictine, and Father Otho Terry, the apologist of Haverstock Hill . . . . The secretary of the Congregation, Father Dangelis, is against you. You will be crushed . . . . . . useless struggle . . . . . . spoken of as a certitude at Cardinal Manueci's . . . . . . Do not expect me to help you. I cannot and I would not if I could, for frankly I consider your book an outrage . . . . . . our old friendship . . . . . . the strictest confidence . . . . . ."

The letter fell from his hand.

Catholic Expansion had been denounced at Rome and was about to be put on the Index . . . denounced! Bennett of Laurium! A pontiff to the finger tips. Stately, revered, magnificent, a man to whom dogma was as the breath of his nostrils. Dom Kenyon he only knew as a profound scholar, the author of historical works ruth-

lessly exposing the fallacies of the Reformation parti-
sans, battering down the lies of Protestant polemics.
Otho Terry was a fiercer enemy still, a man who fought
from lust of battle. An able speaker, a subtle logician,
a bigot who was too clever to show it, he would have
lit the fires of the Inquisition tomorrow had the power
been his, ay, and have gone to the flames himself for his
own convictions.

Little doubt that even these three were carrying out
the vengeance of others, perhaps more powerful than
themselves, who wished to strike in the dark.

Let them—he would fight. Fight! Fight!

The priest rose to his feet as though about to encounter a foe in hand-to-hand combat, almost shouting
the word in a tone of defiance and anger. He turned, as
after quick preliminary knock, the landlady appeared
on the threshold.

"Why, Father, you've not rung yet for me to clear
tea, I thought as how you'd forgotten . . . Lor', it's not
touched and all stone-cold too . . . how dark you've let
it get in here!"

XII

They sat upon a bench beneath the old cedar tree at the
bottom of the lawn. All were busy and the sharp click
of knitting-needles mingled with the sound of voices, a
little subdued as are even the accents of those who have
made the convent their home.

"Nobody could long for a change more than myself. I have made it a matter of penance and prayer."

"Indeed I don't think I could be professed if Father Cassilis were to profess me."

"Hush, Celestine," said Mother Wenburg, "you really must learn to control your mode of expression, and to be less impetuous." She had long attempted to direct the conversation into other channels but seeing that her novices could speak of nothing else, at last she determined to allow their tongues free play on the burning topic, consoling herself with the thought that perchance once one and all had thoroughly discussed the matter and relieved their minds any further talk could be more easily checked on future occasions.

Celestine, a woman with pinched features and thin bloodless lips, moved restlessly. "Well, Mother" she replied, "It's quite true. Anyhow Monsignor has already professed me." She had not the eyes of a mystic, but she was rather one of those persons who, becoming followers of any scheme or movement, must in order to attract notice push every detail to excess, and so often appeared more prominent than the thinkers and the initiators themselves. Now that the convent was electric with discontent, and some mysterious telepathy had organised a regular revulsion against the chaplain, he had no bitterer opponent, no more freely spoken advocate for his removal than Sister Celestine.

"One word more," continued the novice-mistress in tones somewhat more severe than her wont. "Ample has been said upon an unpleasant subject. If we were as eager to obtain as much good from the ministrations as we are ready to criticise the minister, few of us would not be already far advanced on the high way of perfection."

There was silence for a little while.

A white ball of wool rolled off the lap of one of the knitters and fell on to the green grass. From behind a neighbouring shrub a large black cat, the favourite of the Prioress, darted out and with a sudden sharp tap sent the luckless wool dancing across the lawn, unwinding itself in a snowy trail as it went. When puss had been driven away and the ball quickly recovered by its owner, the trifling incident relaxed the tension of the recreation and the air was filled with laughter, quiet, and complacent, albeit rather shrill and sexless.

Veronica, walking in the next pergola, heard the sound with a shudder of acute annoyance. How entirely self-ish the novices were to sit and spend their time in such idle chatter and amusement! It seemed to her that one might as well jest at a sickbed as frivol when the house was plunged in such a crisis. But novices are always thoughtless. It is only after the profession they learn the realities of convent life. A brood of callow birds cackling would have aroused in her the same emotions. What were they talking about? Their sisters, and the plaster images of saints they loved to put up, their pi-ous pictures and manuals.

They were mere children who had exchanged the nursery for the chapel, dolls for statues of the Virgin and S. Joseph. Their love of dressing up, of gauds and tinsel, found an outlet in the vestments of a priest, in the copes and chasubles of a celibate. She remembered how one young novice had actually so far forgotten herself as to clap her hands upon seeing the high altar garlanded and aglow with candles for some feast.

There was no depth in these girls, said Veronica to herself, feeling a vast air of superiority. If Father Cassilis would but leave them their external superfluities, they would reck little if he took the whole core out of their religion, if Christ were made a phantasm, more lifeless more unreal than a pasteboard puppet on a stage of marionettes.

Most of them she supposed had come to the convent pure girls unflecked by the world. There was Ursula who had belonged, as she knew, to a large family, six sisters and five brothers. She could picture their essentially commonplace home somewhere in a southern suburb, a road of villas all exactly alike, all absolutely banal and uninspiring with grandiose names, "The Acacias" or "The Laburnums," or, if the builder's ideas moved in court circles, "Blenheim" or "Balmoral". The genteel mother and her daughters whose goal was matrimony until the youngest suddenly declared she would take the veil.

How Flaubert's soul would have sickened at their life, in what biting truth would he have written them down! The novice's days at home must have been deadly dull. Breakfast at eight every morning, for the brothers were in the city, idle and immature clerks, and there would be the 8.48 train to catch without fail. The routine of housework, the shopping in the High Street, the middle day dinner, Sunday's remnants hashed or stewed and eked out with potatoes, the eventless afternoon only to be filled in by silly novels from the circulating library round the corner or sillier gossip with women leading exactly similar lives, high-tea and for an exciting evening bridge played without stakes or a year old play at a second-rate theatre.

XIII

"What you tell me does not surprise me in the slightest . . . I can follow the psychological process perfectly. You are spiritually sick. You lack the power of concentration. You say that when you meditate your thoughts are disturbed and violated by the recollection of men you knew in the world, that mundane and even sinful ideas mingle with your prayers, with your very adoration of the figure of the Christ . . . I can imagine nothing more horrible . . . Lunacy comes to you in the guise of prayer. It is disgusting . . . but you have encouraged it all yourself, you have paved the way for this infection, this disease, it is nothing else. You have by your reading, by your trend of exotic ideas, created an atmosphere, a habit of mind which is fundamentally bad and absolutely distasteful . . . As for your mysticism, this mixture of the erotic and religious, it is unusual, dangerous to the last degree. Compared with sane devotion it is as a fever by the side of health. I will lend you a book which may help you. Inge's *Christian Mysticism*. If you pay attention to the brief passages I have pencilled, especially those dealing with Sufiism and this hysterical dreaming, in which you have so freely indulged, it may show you the utter folly, the horror of it . . . . I forbid you to practise any mortification of any kind whatsoever, and you are to restrict your fasts to those absolutely required by rule. Until your next confession your subject of meditation will be the words of the Apostle Paul: 'If we live in the Spirit, let us also walk in the Spirit'. . . . . . For your holy penance you will say the 'Veni Creator Spiritus' once daily until your next confession . . . . Et ego te absolvo a peccatis tuis in nomine . . . . Passio Domini nostri . . . . . . Amen."

XIV

She flung herself violently on the bed.

Her cheeks were hectic and fevered, her eyes dry and aching with unshed tears, she moaned hoarsely as she writhed and shivered from head to foot.

"They have taken away my Lord!"

It was earliest dawn, in the half-light dew glittered on the shadowy grass, but no bird had begun to sing, not even a wind's breath rustled the trees in the mysterious garden: all was still and silent. Magdalen knelt before the empty Sepulchre. The stone, sealed and very great, had been rolled away: the tomb was empty. As the first beams of the sun rose in the faded sky they touch the glory of her Titian hair, and lit an aureole around the head of the weeping courtesan.

But she was not to lament overlong. For anon did not her Beloved stand by her and cry "Mary!"

Veronica felt as tho' she also were wailing over a mystic grave, lone and desolate. But for all her woe and agony none came to whom she might cling and call Rabboni.

They had taken away her Lord indeed.

And the empty sepulchre was her life.

Was it empty? Or did there lurk in the dim recesses dead men's bones? The skeletons of love!

Nocturno Itinere Non Intermisso

NOCTURNO itinere non intermisso . . . not omitting journeys by night . . . comitatu equitum . . . accompanied by 30 cavalry he reached the sea . . . the toneless voice of the boy translating Caesar with an occasional stumble and hesitancy sounded even more monotonous than usual, and the curt uninteresting sentences of the *Civil War* seemed, if possible, duller and more soporific than their wont on that hot July afternoon. Through the broad-silled pseudo-Gothic window that opened on a corner of the headmaster's garden came the fragrance of hollyhocks and roses; the golden sunshine full of warmth recklessly plashed colour over the pale distempered walls, hung with anaemic maps, infrequent and awry; from the distant close sounded the regular thud of batting and the clear young voices of three or four practicing at the nets; now and then the gravel scrunched smartly for a second under the firm quick tread of a master passing to his form room or returning home after 1st hour; somebody stopped a moment and spoke to the marshal, whose gruff unmistakable voices answered brusquely in a few grumpy words; the great school clock, whose dial showed gilt hands that branched out high like an old shop sign from the chapel wall, gave a preliminary throb, and then solemnly, sedately, sounded two reverberating strikes, the half-hour; there promptly followed a series of sharp little cries and a noise of rapid running feet as some loiterers, who had lingered overlong at the parapet to watch the flannelled heroes of their house, scattered in anxious haste and fled pell-mell towards their respective classes; then stillness again and the drowsy slumberous silence of a midsummer afternoon. A pot-bellied brown velvet bee who had just swaggered from the tremulous trumpet of the tall Canterbury bells hovered in the window, looped the room and softly buzzed away. An angry bluebottle began to buzz intermittently against a low pane.

Navemque frumentariam conscendit . . . and he went on board a corn-ship . . . It suddenly struck Rollo how ugly young Hewett really was with his bovine neck, gaping mouth, wide nostrils, and stolid features that wore such a worried look as he blurted out, now in an unequal rush, now haltingly slow, the Tale of Pharsalus. Two ink-splotched hands held the book close to his spectacled eyes, and when he read a line or phrase of fogged and forgotten . . . . . . he shuffled uneasily from one foot to the other. Under the spell of the narrative most of the class had sunk into a state of apathy, and when Rollo glanced round the 15 boys he noticed that only professional and despised swotters such as Palma minor and [. . .] intent upon their Moberly. Dick Banstead indeed, who sat opposite him across the room was leaning back with almost ostentatious languor. The inevitable smile just curled his lips, and as usual he had half-closed his great dark eyes. Rollo looked with admiration and affection at the dear olive skin, the black black head, which seemed as if it could not by any possible chance be dishevelled or disarrayed even by the loudest muddiest scrum or the tallest header into the baths. He liked his friend's slim little figure, the newly washed trousers deftly hitched up showing unwashed socks, the low immaculate colour and stiff gleaming cuffs.

Dick—"Dandy Dick" as he was dubbed by Harold, the Upper Fourth Maths man, who in private life imagined, like the heathen of old, a vain thing to wit that he was possessed of histrionic talent, and in company with other shameless and purblind amateurs was accustomed at spasmodic intervals especially at Xmastime to inflict the badly-acted dregs of French's catalogue on audiences long-suffering in the name of charity—Dick Banstead had quite a following amongst the exquisites of the Faith vaguely troubled with the immature D'orsayism of adolescence, when the careless happy state of thick square boots, grubby hands, pockets teeming with chaotic rubble, rapidly trying to give way to the considerations of polo collars, the exact set of a tie, and the nice conduct of the first walking-stick. If Dick were less good at games than he was his fellows would probably have shown some resentment at his natiness but this although always in evidence had ever been discreet to a degree, and boys forgive much, even what they cannot understand, to a member of the

101

Second Fifteen who is sure of his cap in the summer. Besides Banstead was chummy with at least three of the Olympian Sixth, who had been seen walking arm in arm with him more than once, and standing him strawberries in the tuck-shop or meringues and ices at Fanconi's, the little Swiss confectioners, an establishment extensively patronised by the School.

Nobody could help liking Dick and he was such a thorough good sort; at all events the only person ever to fall foul of him had been "grubster" Olivant, out of whose form he and Rollo had made a happy passage only the term before last to the region of the Lower Fifth. Olivant, a lean-jawed libellous tyrant with bad teeth and sour breath, was notoriously négligé as regards sartorial embellishments. Probably his own gaunt rawboned figure and ungainly angles would have defied the utmost craft and skill of a Sackville Street tailor. His trousers seemed eternally creased and raddled beyond all pressing; the waistcoat, furrowed in a thousand folds, glinted with more than one shiny spot; his linen was by no means sumptuously clean, and he had a way of suddenly shorting down one cuff to nip off some frayed edge with a pair of nail-scissors which he used to carry folded in his pocket; his gown was the mustiest in the School; whilst the obviously made up ties he affected had become a legend and landmark. They were invariably glossy and continually new, invariably of some abnormally bright colour, orange, cerulean or coquelicot. A garish red satin he particularly affected, and rumour, stoutly contradicted by his house, said that he had once even donned a species of neck gear distinguished by floral decorations. His form used to speculate on how many ties he wore a term, and at what weird clandestine shop he bought them.

From this very first coming into his form Olivant had had a down on Rollo and Dicky, on Dicky in particular. To do the man justice he despised the boy as a budding coxcomb, and would have been glad to have seen him thoroughly ragged by the rest. When he understood that Banstead was far too popular for anything of the sort, and what is more was quite well able to hold his own, his dislike intensified.

The trickiest of Latin conditionals, the most insular of Greek verbs, the hardest chapter in political history, descended in an avalanche of questions on Dicky's devoted head. Mistakes were met with mockery, hesitation with lumbering sarcasm that never failed to gain its round of sycophantic laughter from a little coterie of official flatterers, whose heads had to be punched in grand style directly after the lesson. Even when Dick's construal was perfect and his answers quite correct they were cavilled at with waspish insistence that became all the more acrid as it seemed to have little or no effect. Had the boy not had grit, a sense of humour, and electric vitality he would almost have succumbed under the continual persecution, for it was little else. As they wrote their weekly Latin or Greek prose in form, for half-an-hour and more at a time Olivant would sit glowering at him in grim silence, a heavy frown on his face, his ragged moustache bristling with discoloured tutt. At last one Nov. afternoon just before the gas jets were lit he eyed Banstead slipping a paper along to

Rollo under the cover of an atlas. It was signed, and on it was discovered a clever but libellous caricature of Olivant as a filthy fakir, clad in a loin-cloth neatly coloured with red ink, repudiating a bath and a cake of Pear's soap with the words "Odi Persian apparatus." Dicky was incontestably sent up to the Head-master, who being in a bad temper flogged him then and there for gross impertinence, whilst Olivant himself had the pleasure of bending Rollo over a form and giving him eight with a fives bat on that part which schoolboys allude to by a crude monosyllable, and which Balzac says the angels are created without, and the boy felt more than a little sick after it, for the punishment was anything but a light one—meted out with a vigorous and practiced hand.

But that was all months ago and as he sat here in the comparative calm of VY Rollo felt he could afford to look back if not with forgiveness at least without any mad lust for revenge even on Olivant, whom now he never saw save in the distance and afar off. But how they had mugged that Xmas exam, to escape his clutches! And both he and Dicky had been resting on their oars, as far as work was concerned at any rate, ever since.

Qua re impetrate . . . Which thing having been accomplished . . .

Dicky gave a little yawn, opened his eyes wide for a minute and smiled across at Rollo.

Rollo smiled back. He had never seen anyone look quite so frankly bored. Last night when, with a tremendous air of determination, they had opened their Caesars, Dicky of a sudden declaimed vehemently against Caius Julius as a "sultry old blighter" and vituperated with more than usual ardour the *Bellum Civile* as the dullest and stuffiest of all his works and ways, an opinion in which Rollo was not slow to concur. The chances of their being called up to construe were then rightly considered; Rollo had been put on the day before yesterday, and Dicky owing to certain notes written in cryptic minuscules on the tiniest slip of thinnest foreign paper had acquitted himself with glory earlier in the week; it was more than improbable that Whitmore would pitch on either so soon after. The *Commentaries* were closed with a bang and work relegated to the background. Dicky produced his cigarette case and a couple of cigarettes were carefully smoked close to the open window, having enclosed themselves with many precautions on an ample window seat well behind the curtains. Rollo softly dropped a good third of his into the garden with a secret resolve to steal out later and bury it in the soft mud of a flower-bed. The usual etiquette was observed: on being offered another he casually replied "not just yet, old thing," and Dicky himself, when he had elaborately finished his first, half-opened the case and replaced it in his pocket, murmuring something about "keeping a fag for the way home." So they lounged side by side looking at the countless stars of the summer night scattered like gold dust over the dark blue cavernous sky, the Bears great and little, the Milky Way, Sagittarius and the proud queen of Cepheus on her throne of ivory. The two boys in desultory sentences discussed odds and ends of school gossip, and Dicky asked if Rollo thought he had any chance of the home eleven when they went over, and would Harding get his twenty-two colours for certain? This led to a circumstantial review of Dicky's somewhat chequered career, and as details not normally known were exchanged, voices lowered significantly, and the two heads, the dull gold and the dark, came close together.

Yet with all their friendship and their near confidence, for all the many evenings Dick was round at Rollo's place or Rollo went over to Dicky's, ostensibly to turn into native wisdom or to wrestle with the archaisms of Homeric sagas—it was noticeable that as the dread time of examinations approached these nights became more and more infrequent until at the penultimate week they had ceased entirely and both Rollo and Dicky would then be found working separately, each on his own—with fevered brow and anguished eyes— for all their walks and rambles and cycle rides, Rollo felt that, although of the whole school Dicky probably liked him best, he could never break through a certain wall of reserve which persisted between them. There was something tenuous but opaque that continually baffled him. He wondered if Dicky had perhaps interests and affinities which escaped him entirely, which he was too dense to understand and appreciate. When they were together these thoughts worried his mind and he would look rather curiously at his friend seeking a solution of the riddle. Maybe he decided it was all just his imagination. And then when Dicky turned his big dark eyes full on him and looked him straight in the face his own eyes dropped and he flushed self-consciously. Yet even whilst they were sprawling together on the broad window sill with its heap of cushions or lying on the old sofa that was so prominent a piece of furniture in Rollo's tiny den he could never put his arm so caressingly around Dicky's shoulders, he could never feel so utterly and completely intimate with him as he did with Hilary Vickels.

Sometimes as they sat working at the little square table when the maroon serge had been neatly folded and put on one side, and the shiny American cloth underneath was heaped with numerous exercise books, pens, pencils, rubbers, Page's edition of the *Odes* in its bright scarlet binding, and a dull backed but friendly old Bohn, or if it were an English night Hales' *Longer English Poems*, and maybe *The Tempest* or *Richard II* sandwiched between the ungrammatical introduction of yeasty notes of some academic pedant or school inspector, whilst Dicky was chasing an elusive word through the pages of Smith's smaller Dictionary, Rollo leaning back would look rather curiously at his friend seeking a solution of the puzzle.

His beloved House chum. Dick was really rather a mystery somehow . . .

"Dolt! Dolt! Sluggard! Correct him, Gore!"

Rollo gave a start, and flushed hotly. He took a swift glance the open page before him trying hard to remember the last words which were indistinctly buzzing in his brain.

The Between Maid

MIDNIGHT, murky, dank and drear, when all is hushed and still, is always thought of by romantic poets and romantic people as the ghostly hour at which

> Roused from their slumbers,
> In grim array the grisly spectres rise,
> Grin horrible, and, obstinately sullen,
> Pass and repass, hushed as the foot of night.

Perhaps our imaginations have been influenced by *Hamlet*, and if we think or speak of ghosts our subconscious at once pictures the chill, dark battlements of Elsinore, where the silence is only broken by the lonely footfall of the sentinels, the quick "Who's there? Stand," and the few brief words they exchange, "'Tis now struck twelve." "'Tis bitter cold," and the terror of the watch as the shadowy phantom figure, "the Majesty of buried Denmark," stalks past in awful silence. We think of Hamlet on the next night, venturing to the haunted keep, to discover if haply it be indeed his royal father's spirit, "doom'd for a certain term to walk the night," and his question: "What hour now?" to which Horatio answers: "I think it lacks of twelve:

> Then it draws near the season,
> Wherein the spirit held his wont to walk."

In building up his atmosphere for those ghost-scenes which so powerfully open that play, considered by many the masterpiece of the world's greatest tragedies, how insistent is Shakespeare upon the hour of midnight, upon darkness, and isolation, and cold.

Sceptics have mockingly asked: "And why do apparitions never appear during the day-time?" The answer is: "They do."

I have known many instances of apparitions seen in full daylight, and in some sense they can be more alarming than the dim midnight spectre. Perhaps the most extraordinary and the most undisputable of all was the case of No. 15 Redcliffe Road, Clifton Down, Bristol.

In the good old days, forty years ago, houses were by no means difficult to get. No matter what you wanted, whether it were a cottage or a mansion, within a very few weeks you might be sure of finding it. Which sounds like a fairy tale.

When, after the death in India of her husband, Colonel Conroy, Mrs. Conroy returned to England with her three daughters, and decided to settle in Clifton, where her family had lived whilst she was a girl, a month had not passed before she secured a long lease of No. 15 Redcliffe Road, Clifton Down. The agents had been enthusiastic, and the house in question proved all that was claimed for it.

Standing well back from the road, it was situated in one of the best and quietest parts of Clifton and the rent asked was remarkably reasonable for such a favourite district. In fact, it was so reasonable that Mrs. Conroy insisted upon the premises being thoroughly vetted before she took possession. But not a fault was to be found. Even Jonson, Mrs. Conroy's maid, expressed herself as perfectly satisfied with her quarters.

The furniture was soon got out of store, and the move was accomplished quickly and easily; as moves were accomplished in those happy days. The Conroys settled very comfortably in their new home.

The only trifling difficulty was that the housemaid could not take up her post as soon as they wished. It would be nearly a month before she could come, lamented Mrs. Conroy, who dwelt incessantly upon the necessity for engaging a "temporary". Miss Conroy and her two sisters, Miss Jessie and Miss Annie, did not see the need for anything of the sort. But Mrs. Conroy shook her head.

"It will be just like mother to go and get some daily girl from the registry office without telling us, or saying a word to anyone," Miss Jessie warned them.

Accordingly Miss Conroy was not so much surprised as annoyed, when on returning home one day about noon she passed on the stairs a young girl, in a pink print dress, who was most busily engaged with a brush and pan sweeping away as if for dear life. Miss Conroy only gave her a glance as she passed, but somehow she formed a most unfavourable impression.

The new maid was distinctly untidy and dowdy, not to say sluttish. Her cap was soiled and all awry, and Miss Conroy felt something almost like a shudder of disgust, and hurried up to her room. "Whatever can mother be thinking of?" she said, as she unpinned her hat, "to engage a slattern like that! She's only fit for a third-rate lodging-house. What will anyone say if she happens to open the door to them should Jonson be upstairs? She really is a most horrible, untidy Cinderella to be about a place. Round-shouldered, too, practically humped-backed, poor thing. And such a white, unhealthy face, enough to give one the creeps."

The next day Miss Annie caught sight of the new maid, who, upon seeing her, slithered away downstairs giving a hideous grin over her shoulder as she closed the door behind her. "Really, I believe that girl Mamma's got is half-witted," said Miss Annie rather crossly to her elder sister. "A pasty-faced creature grimacing like a Cheshire cat. She's not all there, I'm convinced."

One morning, about half-past eleven, when the Conroys had been in their new house a week or so, I took the privilege of an old and intimate friend, to pay an informal call, to wish them a pleasant settling in. My good friend Jonson answered the door, and greeted me with her usual frank and ample smile. "Well, Jonson," I said, "and how are you all getting on? I only came to ask if there is anything we can do for you. I am not going to intrude." "Oh, do come in for a minute, sir," she answered, "the young ladies are out, but the mistress is in the morning-room, and she will be delighted to see you. You know how fond she is of a bit of a chat in the morning."

"If you are sure—" I began, and then stopped short. For just behind the prim and precise Jonson, so close indeed as to be peering over her shoulder, I saw a most repulsive-looking and dishevelled tweeny-maid, the sort of girl I could not have supposed Mrs. Conroy would have allowed in her house for a moment.

A dirty pink frock, a smudged and smutted apron, long a stranger to the laundry, a grimy cap trolloping over a tangle of uncombed hair, all looked singularly out of place at the front door of that spick-and-span house, close beside a maid who might just have stepped out of a bandbox.

The girl gave a sort of ugly grin at my obvious amazement, and in a moment had slipped away through the red baize door at the back of the hall. I caught a look of surprise on Jonson's face, and made haste to answer, "Why, of course, if you are sure I shan't be disturbing Mrs. Conroy."

That lady greeted me warmly, only too glad to secure a listener, when she had so much to say. In fact, the conversation was in the nature of a monologue dealing with the numberless perils and adventures of a move.

On the following Sunday, after the midday dinner, Mrs. Conroy and her two younger daughters drove out to pass the rest of the day with some cousins who lived on the other side of Clifton Suspension Bridge, in Leigh Woods.

The cook and Jonson were given the afternoon off from teatime, and Miss Conroy, seeing that the evening was remarkably warm and fine—it was early September—decided to go to church. She was on her way downstairs to get some hot water to wash before going out, but when she reached the hall she heard somebody bustling about pretty briskly in the basement. Supposing that either the cook or Jonson had got back, she called out, "Oh, Jonson, would you bring me up a can of hot water, please, I am going to church."

She waited five or six minutes, and then, thinking that she had not been heard, for the noise of somebody moving to and fro was still quite distinct, she went down to the basement herself to fetch the water. The kitchen door was half-open, and when she pushed it wide, to her astonishment she saw, her back turned towards her and apparently busy at the range, the girl in the pink print dress. "What on earth are you doing here?" she inquired in a loud, indignant voice.

The girl swung round with a horribly impudent leer on her drawn, white face, and without a word of explanation or apology, scuttled off into the adjoining scullery, a room from which there was no exit. Thoroughly incensed, Miss Conroy, thinking, "Ah, I've caught you now," followed.

What was her amazement when she found that the scullery was absolutely empty. A great wave of nausea seemed to surge up over her, and (she told me), "I simply turned tail and ran upstairs."

When she reached the landing she paused to recover her breath, but to her absolute horror she saw grinning and mowing from outside the window, thirty feet from the ground, the face, white and loathsome as the belly of a fat, bloated slug, of the between-maid, whom she had left in the kitchen a minute ago. "How I got out of the house I don't know," she used to say. She managed to reach the next door, and pulled the bell violently. They found her in a dead faint in the porch.

An illness followed, and it took several months at Brighton before she really recovered. As may be supposed, Number 15 Redcliffe Road was promptly vacated by the Conroys, who were fortunate enough to find in a short time a house which was untroubled and clean.

Years afterwards Miss Conroy often said: "Would you believe that the sight of an ordinary maid in a pink print frock, even in the middle of the morning, will give me quite a start still?"

Although it had all been most carefully hushed up, and it proved exceedingly difficult to get anyone to say anything, some very odd facts came to light concerning No. 15 Redcliffe Road. Fifty or more years before, there lived in the house an old woman who was reputed to be immensely wealthy, although she existed like a beggar, and when she was seen, she was clothed in a gown little better than rags. She further bore a very evil reputation.

There was only one maid in the house, a half-witted creature, a hunch-backed drab always dressed in the cheapest pink print frock. Some whispered that she was the beldarne's natural daughter. Be that as it may, it was known that the old harridan starved and beat her, and used her with fiendish cruelty. In the end the wretched girl drowned herself in a large reservoir at the bottom of the garden.

Fearful stories were told of the woman's deathbed. After Holy Communion had been administered, it was found, when she was dead, that she had vomited out the Sacred Elements at the foot of the bed. Rumour had it how on that very day, dark elusive shapes and shadows had been half-seen in the passages and on the stairs.

That the family who took 15 Redcliffe Road when the Conroys had broken their lease did not stay a full month I personally know, whilst the tenants who followed left most abruptly within even a shorter time. This sort of thing could not be kept quiet. Ugly stories spread, and it was impossible to contradict them. Nobody would look at the house.

The last I heard of it was that it had been taken by a large removal firm as a furniture depository. That was some years ago, but certain I am that even today it remains empty, save for the one occupant—the between-maid.

In Spite of the Fitful Promise

IN spite of the fitful promise of the sun a little before
midday, when it seemed almost possible for anyone
walking down the High Street to be optimistically per-
suaded that perhaps after all it might turn out quite
warm and fine, this October afternoon proved wild
and stormy enough with great tempestuous gusts and
a quick scud of cold pattering rain, as the darkness
hurried on over the monochrome of the featurelessly
stark sky, against which the three tapering spires of the
Cathedral seemed to peer up gaunt and grim for all
their tracery and comeliness, each exquisite detail now
merged and shadowed in the swift onset of the autumn
gale and the night beyond. Across the Close itself there
capered and galloped a restless rout of thin shrivelled
leaves, leaping and falling in a wild whirling lavolta to
the whistling of the wind, the creaking and groaning of
the old elm trees, careering over the green, up and down
the neatly gravelled paths; then suddenly subsiding in
large untidy heaps scattered here and there, only to stir
again the next moment and be tossed helter skelter to
every quarter of the compass.

Undeniably it was a dreary landscape beneath that pale hard sky, so dreary that only those who knew it familiarly and had long stored up unforgettable memories of its beauty could have guessed how lovely it would be again when the July sun was hot upon the lush grass, thick and smooth as that of Oxford lawns in the nooks of quiet colleges, a fleecy carpet chequered with the shade of rusting foliage, when the gardens which fronted those old grey houses circling the Close were a veritable radiance of flowers, scarlet and amandine, saffron and gold, turquoise and gentian, purple, ivory, jet, blood and flame; or again on a winter morning with the nip of frost in the air, the ground muffled in deep untrod snow, whose great flakes plumped silently and soft as wool from the overladen branches or clustered tenderly about the feet of the Gothic Queen, diamonded with rime, who clasping close to her bosom her little Babe, smiled from the right royally canopied and foliate niche that topped the vast West door.

Fair indeed on a summer day, all life and colour and warmth, fair in midwinter when wrapped in the stillness of virginal snow, on this autumnal afternoon the Close seemed inexpressibly melancholy and depressing.

At any rate, so Miss Hevingman thought as at four-fifteen on Thursday, 8th October, her features lowering in a steady look of annoyance and disapproval—no rare visitor there—she gazed sourly enough from the bay of her drawing-room windows, which the raindrops had already begun to sprinkle with their sharp petulant patters that coursed in quick little crooked runnels down the glass. Although alone she even gave somewhat ve-

118

hement expression to her feelings, which, to do her justice, she never attempted to conceal in any company or in any place. "This is pleasant to come back to, indeed," she muttered in a tone of infinite disgust. "I have never seen the Close looking more dreary, never."

And if Miss Hevingman had never seen the Close looking drearier than today it is well-nigh certain that there was nobody else who could pretend to boast a more intimate knowledge of its potentiality for cheerlessness and gloom, since during nine and fifty years she had had ample opportunities of contemplating it at her fullest leisure, day in and day out, save indeed on the rare occasions of formal visits to distant relatives, as also during the annual solemnity of a month spent at Weymouth, Buxton, or Bath, which in recent years had been extended to one of those popular Swiss resorts where they provide chocolate-box scenery for the benefit of English tourists, snow-capped mountains, a lake, a blue sky, and above all, the inevitable appendage of a Protestant clergyman, who on Sunday or at a convenient hour reads with sweet unction and chaste confidence an abbreviated form of Morning Prayer in the deserted salon of the hotel.

Nearly sixty years ago Martha Hevingman had been born in the Deanery, which faces the north side of the Cathedral. It is a fairly impressive house with an air of solid Jacobean comfort and spaciousness few houses have been able so successfully to retain in these overcrowded and Bolshevist days. By strangers it is inevitably mistaken for the Palace—which is, in fact, a modern and appalling structure of hybrid hideousness at Applegarth, some eight miles out of Melchester on the Wilsthorpe road. Yet the Deanery indeed is far more deserving of the title, for it has loyally entertained more than one English king. In the Great Chamber—a wonderful old room with an oriel window, linen-patterned walls, tall mirrors and tapestried doors, a huge stone fireplace and mighty chimney, stout oak beams, carved transoms, an uneven undulating floor—they still show the bed where Charles I slept or waked on the night after Naseby, a gargantuan bed, plumed like a tragic hero, with heavy columns, dark velvet curtains powdered with quaint devices and heraldic medallions that hang in faded folds now, but whose rich broideries of gold and forest of fringe were once untarnished and new. Here also, thirty years after, reposed a very different occupant—the blue-eyed whey-skinned Louise Renee de Penancoët de Cornouaille, lodged there for a night by her royal lover to whom Dean Oldys (*ob.* 1683) showed himself far more complaisant a courtier than did his brother Ken on a similar occasion. But this story was not generally repeated as being unsuitable to the atmosphere of the Close.

The Deanery had even the distinction, which is probably by no means unique in the twentieth century, of refusing hospitality to a King. For when William of Nassau graciously signified his intention of passing a night in Melchester, good Dr. Jeremy Powell, the non-juring successor of urbane Dean Oldys, flatly refused to receive the Orange usurper and incontinently locked up his doors, an action which led to his suspension not many weeks later.

Assuredly no such indecorous incident could possibly have taken place at the Deanery under the rule of the Very Reverend Philip Hevingman, an ecclesiastical mandarin sleek in person and smooth of tongue, who had always piqued himself upon "gentlemanly moderation in all things" and "due consideration for the honest convictions of others," muntrums which he had repeated with such success in all circumstances that he stepped from preferment to preferment and added sinecure to sinecure until it seemed not wholly impossible that the converted mitre of Canterbury itself might be within reach of his fat podgy fingers, whilst all the while the truculent high church papers roundly accused him of heresy, if not flat unbelief, and his nickname "Pliable Phil" was merrily echoed throughout the length and breadth of England. When he died—which he did with obvious reluctance—he was held up in flatulent sermon and soppy memoirs as a pattern and a model of the sound English churchman, a true son of Ecclesia Anglicana, the pietist whose motto had ever been *ne quid nimis*, san of course (but this was not hinted at) in regard to the pelf so substantially accumulated during his long career of indetermination and vapid uselessness.

Pliable Phil had, in fact, left his one surviving child, Martha, comparatively wealthy, and it was in tacit consideration of her that even after she had perforce vacated the Deanery, a terrible blow to her importance, she continued by a species of social simony to rule the Close with a rod of iron, or it might be more accurately said, a rod of gold. Not that she was foremost

121

in subscriptions of generosity in charity, but Martha Hevingman's money had in the course of years grown to be a formidable legend before whose thrall she expected both bishop and butcher-boy to bow. She well knew her power, and she not infrequently abused it, secure against any very active resistance in sleepy old Melchester.

Staunch allies of her income were an itching curiosity, no small disregard for truth—this trait was an obvious inheritance from her father—a smudgy imagination, the outlook of an intensely sexual woman to whom respectability denied gratification, and a bitterly acidulated tongue.

Upon meeting Miss Hevingman for the first time one was aware of something unusual yet not entirely unprepossessing, and it was only gradually that you realised her costume recalled the mode of nearly forty years ago. This was especially the case of an afternoon when she affected a narrow skirt of black satin or black brocade embellished with three deep flounces and a sweeping train, In the house a white lace cap of some size crowned the dark hair that was beginning to be heavily streaked with iron grey, an oval broach painted with some Roman contadino clasped the fleecy shawl, long golden drops hung in her ears, her favourite jewels seemed hard red stones, table-cut garnets and round carbuncles.

Miss Hevingman was at the moment impatient and resentful. The weather seemed to her no less than a studied affront. There had not been a visitor—a ring at the bell—since lunch. Perhaps her own self-consciousness whispered now and then how brittle her dignity was, and in consequence she had fallen into the habit of guarding it with too nice a punctilio that led her to suspect covert slights from those who had not intended, and indeed would not have ventured to offend.

On the Wednesday afternoon she had arrived home after her annual absence, which happened this year to have been exceptionally prolonged. The latter half of August and the first fortnight of September she had passed in Switzerland, but not having slept well on one or two nights and complaining that the food did not suit her digestion upon her return to England she was pleased to fancy herself "not quite completely set up," as she phrased it. Her housekeeper was an excellent old servant, and so after writing several sheets of most minute and superfluous instructions to Melchester from her Earl's Court hotel she proceeded in semi-invalid state to Buxton where she religiously drank the waters which she did not need in the slightest, took two good walks every day to restore her perfect health, and in the evening bored to salt tears the unwary flies whom she had managed to entangle in the web of predaceous conversation. The final week was spent at Peterborough, where she enjoyed the double satisfaction of criticising the household arrangements of her hostess, a distant cousin who longed fiercely for her aunt's demise, and of contrasting the Cathedral services with those of Melchester to the infinite advantage of the latter.

"My dear Alice, I cannot imagine why you do not insist upon your parlour-maid being changed by midday. Nothing looks worse, I always think, than a print dress at the door after twelve-o'-clock. Take my word for it, you will never be able to manage your servants properly until they see that you have a sharp eye on all these details. And now the subject has been brought up, you really should speak to them about the amount of gas they waste. I assure you that Millet at home would be quite shocked to see the way they go on. Yes, I know that we have electric light, and, of course, you only have gas. I quite realise how inconvenient it must be. I am sure I have found it most uncomfortable these last few days. Nothing but striking matches, even if one wants to look at one's watch in the middle of the night. I don't know how you would manage if anybody was taken ill . . . But I noticed that the gas was simply flaring in Andrew's study yesterday evening. I just peeped round the door as I was going upstairs to fetch my knitting after dinner. Simply flaring away, that's the only word for it. Yes, naturally I understand that being so near-sighted—and I can't imagine why he doesn't consult a London oculist—he likes to have a good light, but that hardly excuses the extravagance, and it is so dangerous too! And I am sure that Esther won't be back on Tuesday evening until well after ten-o'-clock. You ought to make a strict rule that your maids are in by half-past nine at the latest; you never know what they may have been up to keeping such hours. And I must insist, Alice, that you speak to your cook. The pastry of that apple-tart we had with dinner last night was so heavy that I'm afraid it has started my digestive troubles again. Fortunately I happen to have with me some excellent peppermint tablets Dr. Singer gave me, so we will hope it may be a passing attack. But this afternoon I will just lie down on the sofa in the study and try to get a quiet nap if nobody will please disturb me. Andrew can write his letters later, or use the morning room. I am sure he wouldn't begrudge me the study for half an hour. If you don't like to speak to cook yourself, dear, shall I speak for you? I have so much more experience in administering these little domestic reproofs, she might be more likely to listen to me." And Alice, who was retaining her cook by subtle strategy and gross adulation, would set her teeth and silently pray for patience.

Yes; Miss Hevingman's grand tour had both by reason of its extent and importance partaken of the nature of a triumph. She felt that when she had arrived at Melchester Station at three forty-five yesterday afternoon, and Mr. Croft, the station-master, had greeted her so civilly and respectfully with the usual ritual. "Good afternoon, mum. Glad to have you back after so long. Never looking better in your life, mum." To which she had majestically replied, "Good afternoon. Thank you, Mr. Croft." And he had taken her ticket himself.

There had been no tiresome delay nor difficulty in finding her luggage, and old Malden—advised by a post-card—was punctually awaiting her with his best fly, in the antique depths of which, as she drove out from the Station Yard, up High Street, and through Market Place to climb the incline that leads to the Close, she sat well back so as to be completely lost to view. It was not Miss Hevingman's way to return from a holiday and acknowledge bows and raised hats from behind the windows of a rattling cab. That would be nothing of an entry, and her advent demanded far more ceremony. It was an established custom that on the afternoon following her return she was at home to the numerous female satellites of the Cathedral set, duly forewarned by letter to attend, when they would meet to dole out flattery to their hostess, to compliment her on her appearance, to admire her new gown, drink tea, look at picture post-cards of the hotels where she had stayed and other totally uninteresting views, and, above all retail any items of Melchester history which, true or false, had taken place whilst she was away. On the following morning after Matins in the Cathedral, at which she assisted as a Catholic might have a Mass of Thanksgiving, Miss Hevingman would make a stately progress down the High Street to receive the homage of the shopkeepers, and the salutations of such male folk who usually sauntered there, Archdeacon Rendall, Canon Tabard, Canon Phillimore, Prebendary Shapeste, and gallant old Colonel Cameron.

But it almost seemed as if this afternoon her audience was going to fail her. Such a defection could hardly be accounted for by the weather alone, stormy and wet though it might be. It was unprecedented. And Miss Hevingman was seriously vexed.

"Shall cook toast the muffins now, ma'am, or will you wait a little longer?"

Miss Hevingman turned sharply on the neat white-capped maid with a look of displeasure. She almost felt ashamed to be caught at the window staring out over the Close.

"Let them be toasted at once, Susan, at once. What time is it by the hall clock?"

It was characteristic of Miss Hevingman that although every room in the house contained a clock, and some rooms were even provided with two, it was the old grandfather clock in the hall, gaunt and dark, its face painted with yellow moons, suns and stars, like some fantastic astrological chart, to which appeal was always made when anyone "really wanted to know the time."

The girl glanced through the open doorway where she stood: "Half-past four, ma'am."

"At once then, Susan, at once."

Miss Hevingman advanced towards the tea-table that had so solid an air of comfort and was yet so elegant with its gleaming sides and delicate napery. A small fire burning cheerily on the well-swept hearth before which was placed her ample arm-chair as solemnly imperious as a monarch's throne and in front her own particular square footstool, stout mahogany and beaded wool-stitch, the work of her own hands forty years ago. At the right hand of her chair stood the old fire-screen of grass-green silk, fluted and framed in a formal circle, which could be adjusted to any convenient height upon the slim polished pole.

Slightly warming the tea-pot with water from the bubbling urn, she had already dipped a spoon in the squat japanned caddy when there was a gently apologetic tinkle at the bell and she stopped, spoon poised in mid-air, to listen whose voices could be heard in the hall.

Susan re-appeared at the door.

"Mrs. Tabard and Miss Oakly," she said.

As a matter of fact it was Miss Oakly who first came into the room, and for a moment it might have seemed that she was alone, since Mrs. Tabard had so completely vanished behind her. For she was large and fat, and at the moment breathed heavily as though she had been hurrying rather more quickly than was comfortable for a person of her ample girth. She had a round foolish face, the colour of underdone pastry, which usually assumed an anxious strained stare when you engaged her in conversation however trifling and conventional, the puzzled expression of a person who tries to follow speech in an idiom with which he is little acquainted. Her clothes, which were ill-chosen and ill-made, always gave the idea of being stretched taut over some parts of her body and of hanging loosely in shapeless folds from the rest of her limbs. Whereas she should never have worn anything save the subfusc hues recommended to Oxford undergraduates, she invariably affected colours far too bright for her size. That afternoon wisps of untidy brown hair escaped in every direction from under her large flapping hat.

For all her apparent and real stupidity she was one of the most dangerous women in Melchester. Although by no means rich she had been left in modest comfort, and a toady of the toadies she flattered and sponged upon all who were wealthier than herself whilst she snubbed indiscriminately those she regarded as her social inferiors. Having no interests nor hobbies, no taste for literature, art, music, she devoted herself heart and soul to gossip and incessant tittle-tattle. The little drawing-room of her prim old Georgian house was a very manufactory and hive of scandal, which was carried to and fro with timeless zeal, gathering strength as it deployed abroad. No detail was too paltry, no tale too mean for repetition.

"Well, Charlotte," was Miss Hevingman's stern greeting as she sat very upright in her chair, "I hardly expected to see you at all this afternoon."

"Oh, don't say that, please, dear Miss Hevingman," bleated Miss Oates with a hurried peck at her frostily impassive cheek, "and I have been so looking forward all these weeks—let me see, how long is it? Six, seven weeks,—to seeing you immediately you came back. You can't think how we have all missed you. Only yesterday, or, let me see was it on Monday—no, I suppose it must have been Tuesday because after breakfast Janet came to me to say we had run out of bacon, and would I order some more, and I spoke quite sharply to her, because she ought to make the bacon last out the full week, and Wednesday is ordering-day, not Tuesday, and so I said to her, 'I can't order bacon on a Tuesday, Janet,' and she looked so cross that I thought perhaps I'd better do it after all, so I just stopped into Simpson's, and whoever was coming-out—you'd never guess—old Mr. Crane, and he stopped me to tell me he thought his daughter's cough was rather worse and he was considering whether it wouldn't be advisable for him to take her away somewhere warmer for the winter months, Bournemouth or Torquay, and I told him I knew of some very good rooms at Cromer I stayed in a few years ago, but of course they may have changed hands now, and I really forgot the name of the street, it was number seven or seventeen, and the landlady was a Mrs. Dollies or Ducketh, I remember it began with D and I thought she was rather expensive, but then it was in the summer, their season, you know, and she was a widow, a tall thin woman but very ladylike I must say, and I suppose I was talking to Mr. Crane for quite ten minutes, and I told him, 'Oh, Mr. Crane, do you know Miss Hevingman is coming back on Wednesday?' and he asked me to convey you his respectful compliments, which I thought very polite and gentlemanly of him, and I have always found him very courteous and civil, although my father has often told me that as a boy he remembered his father, who was a coach-handler in Old Town, and he used to swear dreadfully, so I don't think he can have been at all a nice sort of man, and you see, dear Miss Hevingman, I couldn't have forgotten you would be expecting us this afternoon."

"Expecting you, Charlotte, not at all," replied Miss Hevingman, who did not intend to be so easily mollified. "I shouldn't have been surprised if nobody had called, although I am always very glad to see anyone who can spare a quarter of an hour for a cup of tea with me."

By this time Mrs. Tabard, who had been hovering blankly in the background like an uneasy shadow came forward.

"And are you really better, dear, for your change? I must say I am disappointed not to see you looking more robust." She retained Miss Hevingman's hand in the clasp of the two warm black kid gloves, and gazed earnestly into her with an almost pleading expression.

"Never better in my life, Rachel," tartly returned the august lady jerking her hand away with considerable abruptness.

Mrs. Tabard sighed softly, and sank into a chair with a sinuous colubrine movement.

"Ah, yes, of course, you feel that now, but these troubles—it was digestive wasn't it?—come on again so unexpectedly. I suppose you've had to give up bread and potatoes and sugar altogether. Only the other day Dr. Malpas was telling me of one of his patients, who had an attack quite suddenly in the middle of dinner. I believe it was most unpleasant——"

Here fortunately a slight diversion was caused by the entrance of Susan bearing a dome-covered dish piled high with muffins, well-browned, steaming hot, and unctuous with rich melting butter.

Miss Hevingman, who although she herself often liked to descend upon some imaginary ailment and to prophesy the possible advent of worse infirmities, aches, and pains, was not the less apt to be exceedingly irate if any reflection upon her health was ventured by another person, glared stonily at the offending Mrs. Tabard, and after she had filled and handed their cups, with a challenging clink of the tongs ostentatiously dropped three pieces of sugar in her own tea whereas usually she was satisfied with a small lump. Scones and ginger cake she deliberately rejected in favour of the more luscious muffin.

"You would never guess where we have just come from this afternoon," Began Miss Oates with bovine archness. "There is a large drawing-room meeting at the C.M.S. at S. Benet's Vicarage and the Bishop of Koolabe gave an address. Mr. Barret has arranged a small loan exhibition in his study, grass mats, and bracelets, and clubs, and the two assegais and those oblong shield things that hang in Colonel Cameron's hall, the ones he always lends, and bracelets and rings, and bead-necklaces, which I'd never seen before, the most fascinating bead-necklaces, I really felt I should like to wear one myself, and masks, such hideous looking monsters, and a whole witch-doctor's outfit. And he had two of their idols there, just dolls with the stupidest faces, I thought. I wonder whatever they see in them."

"There are people in so-called Christian England today worshipping idols every bit as stupid and ugly," remarked Mrs. Tabard in a grim voice. "I'm not at all sure whether we shouldn't be doing better by trying to convert the heathen at home, before we convert Africans. I sometimes think so."

"Oh, Dr. Holland is in England, is he?" said Miss Hevingman. "I had no idea of that, nor that he was likely to be coming to Melchester. He is such a good man. I might have arranged a little dinner-party if I had known. How long is he staying, Charlotte?"

"Only tonight, I think."

"Then, of course, there's no time. Did you hear if he is stopping with Mr. Barrett?"

"Yes, I asked particularly. The bishop is speaking at Ulverton this evening in the parish hall with lantern slides. It is in support of his native schools. There was a silver collection this afternoon. They must have got over twenty pounds."

"Hardly as much as that," corrected Mrs. Tabard. "It takes a good many sixpences and shillings to make up twenty pounds. Not to mention threepenny bits."

"Threepenny bits? Did you see any? I dare say Jane Taylor would give a three penny bit. I really must say I believe she gets meaner and meaner every day. And if one hints at anything quite kindly, she always declares she can't afford it. She can't afford to support the Restoration Fund, she doesn't subscribe to the library, she never buys a single thing at any of the church bazaars, and I know for a fact that she only has a paper every other morning because I asked Mrs. Cole, who works for her twice a week, Tuesdays and Saturdays, 'Mrs. Cole,' I said, 'does Miss Taylor take *The Daily Mail* every morning?' And she said, 'Oh, no, Miss, *The Express* on Tuesdays and *The Mirror* on Saturdays,' and she regularly has to go out and buy them, so she's not likely to be wrong. I hate such cheese-pairing. Of course it was very sad when her brother died so suddenly, and I shall always maintain that we never did hear the rights of that story. There was something peculiar, depend upon it. I shouldn't be surprised if it came out one day. And no doubt she did lose a certain amount of money then, although probably it wasn't nearly as much as she would have liked us to suppose. She never took me in. And I expected she was only at the C.M.S. this afternoon to get a cheap tea. Not that she got much for her pains, I thought the tea was very poor. I am sure it hadn't been made with boiling water. Nobody even offered me a second cup. And the rock-cake I had was quite stale with hardly any currants in it. A very second-rate affair. And now, dear Miss Hevingman, I am longing to hear all about your stay at Zermatt and your nice visit to Cheltenham, I mean Buxton."

Miss Hevingman, whose temper had been considerably mollified by hearing that her empty drawing room was to be accounted for by a C.M.S. muffin, began to expatiate in detail upon Switzerland.

The Parting of the Ways

DENIS Aldenham paced the platform of the great
station in a strangely discontented frame of
mind. He often suffered from this nameless depres-
sion, and though it passed with time, he had never met
with that which could account for it and cure it. Most
of all, he noticed, it would come over him, darken-
ing all the horizon, when as now he was on the eve
of his return to Oxford. He was now soon due to go
up for his last term, yet he could never feel that he
had come to identify himself thoroughly with the life
of the place. He was not unpopular in his way, and
his set of acquaintances was large and representative
enough to save him from being accounted either a
hermit or a "snug"; his work showed promise for the
coming "schools" and he managed to cut a respectable
figure on the river and in the cricket field: yet none
of his fellow undergraduates claimed him as an intimate friend, and he often noticed that some chance
turn of the conversation seemed to throw him into a
distant and detached mood; and he would often slip
away from a merry party and be heard sporting his oak

for the remainder of the evening. Denis himself felt at times rather keenly that he was somehow out of touch with the views and traditions of men brought up in the same school and the same outward environment as himself: and above all when the conversation chanced to turn, as it does no less frequently in college rooms than elsewhere, on affairs of sex and the common passions and desires of youth. He was no prude, though positively obscene talk had a certain repulsion for him; but woman had never had the least attraction for him, and he never sought, though he did not actually shun, their society. So he realised, though half unconsciously, that he was likely to be a lonely man, as far as intimate relations with either sex were concerned. At school it had not been otherwise: he had at times come under the spell of a kind of romantic hero-worship for boys older than himself and he had occasionally formed strange, unequal, protecting friendships with boys far younger; but many circumstances had stood in the way of his forming any close intimacies. Unequal friendships are looked on askance at public schools: and he had been of too shy and sensitive a nature to let himself attract undue attention.

At home his life was somewhat different: his parents, who exercised little control over him so long as he did not disturb their own comforts, had let him run wild, and he had now and then been strangely drawn to the companionship of keepers, servants and farm-lads on his father's estate: but all his attempts to win their affections—for the rough beauty of these country lads and their simple unaffected ways had an indefinable attraction for him—had failed to meet with any full and genuine response. They had accepted his gifts and his good will, but their own attitude had always been deferential and, in their rough manner, distantly polite: he remained the squire's son, and they could not believe that he meant to offer them anything more than a patronising interest in their lives and pursuits; and he had been too shy to break down their reserve, though he himself could hardly account for the desolating heart-ache which he felt in these, after all, the happiest moments of his early life.

Suddenly, the glare of the electric light, his eyes lighted on a face that touched him oddly. Where had he seen that face before? He recollected vaguely, yet with a kind of hazy reality, that the face belonged to a phantom of his frequent dreams; the face of a boy, four or five years younger than himself, tall, comely, with fair hair and frank, friendly blue eyes, that seemed to say "I am the friend you have been looking for all these weary years: I can give you all that you seem to ask in vain." And here, as he passed in the noise and glare of the busy station, was this same face on the comely figure of a young parcels porter, a youth so handsome that he carried with grace and dignity the coarse, ill-fitting uniform of corduroy, while the unbeautiful peaked and lettered cap, tilted slightly backwards and side-ways on the fair, somewhat wavy hair, seemed only to intensify the pleasing ensemble. Here, despite hard work and poor living, was that perfect, just because not too fault-less, type of athletic English youth which our critics persist in telling us can only be produced in the mill of our gentlemen's schools.

Denis was surprised, although he almost expected to find that the fearless, innocent eyes met his in a quick glance of friendly recognition, accompanied by a genial, unaffected nod. It was as though two comrades who met every day were exchanging an ordinary, hearty token of good-will: and Denis knew it at once for that magnetic attraction of two personalities for each other which sometimes overrides all the conventions and suspicions of a crowded word, "that firm sure-set liking, that boundless will to please" which in the chance meetings of a moment makes old friends of utter strangers. Within a minute's space the wealthy undergraduate and the poor railway porter were chatting familiarly, regardless of the triviality of the indifferent topic of the instant, and the difference in expression which might have set an indefinable barrier between two souls less perfectly in harmony, but so widely severed by the conditions of modern life.

Less than five minutes later the first meeting of Denis Aldenham and Jim Aston was brought to a sudden close by the arrival of the North express: yet not before the latter had accepted an invitation to the theatre for the following evening and a warm grasp of the hand passed between the two. Denis felt impelled to stay in Middletown until the last possible moment, and the evening at the theatre and a modest supper after was followed by another meeting at the station during a slack period of the following morning, at which the two lads pledged each other to correspond frequently and to meet again at the earliest opportunity.

Several times during the term Denis Aldenham came down from Oxford to spend an all too short weekend in Middletown with Jim. Meanwhile he considered how he might befriend his strange chum to the best advantage. He had the instinctive good sense not to attempt to "raise him," and so to spoil the charm of his natural and unconscious refinement by trying to convert him into that unattractive bastard product which is the pride of university extension movements and slum settlements, the "educated working man." Only he concentrated his efforts on the preservation of Jim's singular comeliness of person and character, and to this end he strove to remove him from the most sordid of the conditions which coarsen the labouring youth in our great towns of today, and almost inevitably bring the bonny, healthy lad to a dull and uninviting middle age almost before he has reached years of manhood. Jim, on his eighteen shillings a week, lived alone in a single room in a block of "model" dwellings that was little better than a "black-spot" slum: and from the very fact that Jim, usually so frank in all matters concerning his antecedents and surroundings, had hesitated for a long time before allowing Denis to see his wretched quarters, his friend suspected that there was much that distressed him in the dire necessity that forced him to live in such a place. With some difficulty, for Jim was from first to last unwilling to accept favours beyond the common give-and-take of equal friendship, Denis induced him to make his home with an old nurse of his own, who had a clean and comfortable cottage in a decent street in a near suburb of Middletown: and the lad, with some hesitation, accepted from his friend the small difference in weekly sum for board and lodging which the change cost. When once the step was taken he was obviously relieved and happier: his health grew perceptibly more robust, and his face and figure, Denis was glad to find, became more comely, more charming than ever under the influence of better food and air.

After Jim's removal, the two lads spent as many weekends together as possible in closer union than before; for there was ample room in the cottage for Denis to spend his whole time there, sharing his friend's bed. Now at last both realised, though both at present failing completely to understand, the strange but beautiful mystery that in such a friendship as theirs the passing of the night in chaste but intimate physical contact was as essential a complement of their mutual love as in the common relation of life the union of man and wife.

Meanwhile, the content which Denis found in the frequent intercourse with his affinity stimulated his efforts in his studies at Oxford rather than disturbed them. His own experiences, he discovered, threw a new light on his reading of the classics, especially on certain phases of Greek life, which he had hitherto apprehended only as a strange, sometimes a disquieting mystery. In the stories of Achilles and Patroclus, Heracles and Iolaus, Hadrian and Antonius, in certain of the poems of Anacreon and Meleager and in the sweetest eclogue of Vergil, he saw reflected the romance of his own life: and in his frequent short vacations the murky atmosphere of Middletown became enthused with the delicate sunshine of the Attic seaboard.

By good fortune Denis also lit on certain modern works in his general reading which attempted to explain scientifically to a perverse and stubborn generation this idiosyncrasy of human nature so completely understood by the ancient world and so wilfully ignored and even half-forgotten during centuries of Christian civilisation. From these he learned that his own temperament, though a variation on the normal phrase of the sexual life, was no disease or morbid perversion, as public opinion maintained when it dared face the question at all, but that the passion that inspired his love for Jim could soar, like any other, to the noblest heights of friendship, or to be allowed to be degraded to the lowest depths of lust. It lay in his own hands, then, to make the best or worst of himself and his friend, to convert this wonderful sign of friendship that nature had given him into a blessing or a curse. But did it not rest, after all, entirely on his own will? Could love reach these heights of self-realisation without perfect reciprocity on the part of the beloved, or must his friend be endowed with a similar nature to himself? He fell to wondering, for instance, whether his love could bear the intervention of a woman, and in this case, whether his passion for Jim could be made exalted enough to bear the sacrifice with fortitude and without rupture of the cherished friendship: or would it be subject to the jealousies and disillusionments of a normal passion? Here he sought guidance from the sages, but found none.

He resolutely put away these misgivings, and consciously made his love the inspiration of his work for the present. The spring passed pleasantly in reading well in hand for the June examinations, and in frequently idyllic Sundays spent with Jim on country rambles within reach of Middleton. When the ordeal approached, Denis felt completely nerved to cope with it, and he was confident that he had acquitted himself with credit in the greater number of papers. Near the end came the general paper, in which the specialist has with luck his chief opportunity. As he ran his eye down the questions the blood leapt to his cheeks, for had he set the paper for himself he could not have devised anything that suited better than one of the questions: Compare and contrast the ancient with the modern ideal of friendship. He picked out three or four of the other questions which he liked best, and left a full three-quarters of an hour to do justice to the subject that was nearest to his heart. His pen flew over the paper, and he rose on the stroke of the hour with the knowledge that he had taken a bold step, but filled with the conviction that nothing but gross prejudice on the part of the examiners stood between himself and high honours. He knew that his answer to the last question was a valuable contribution to the sum of human knowledge, but that the valuation lay not within his own power.

After the examination Denis abstained from going near Jim: it seemed almost an impiety to do so while the test of the inspiration of their friendship lay in the balance: and he spent some rather miserable and anxious weeks touring aimlessly about northern France, and finding equally little distraction in the dull gaieties of Norman watering-places and the storied chateaux of Touraine. He returned to Oxford for a late "viva" and stayed there until the results came out. On the fateful day he scanned the list outside the school anxiously from the bottom upwards, according to the usual custom, and his eye searched with increasing anxiety until it rested on his own name at the head of the list—in the first class. In a transport of joy he realised at once what Jim's friendship had done for him, for he knew that the examiners had been kindly disposed towards his most brilliant piece of work, and that but for the fortune of meeting Jim he could never have written that answer.

The same afternoon he received an invitation to tea with his tutor, Mr. Monson, a faded clerical don whose minute linguistic knowledge of the classics was only equalled by his total lack of appreciation of their spirit. Denis had never found Mr. Monson's conversation very sympathetic, but he pitied him today, for the reverend gentleman was obviously more than unusually nervous and incoherent.

"I hasten to congratulate you, Mr. Aldenham," he began, "ah—for the sake of the college on what the examiners assure me is the most brilliant first of the year. At the same time—ah—from a purely personal point of view I should—ah—have hesitated to put so high a value on your general paper, to which, I understand, as matters stand, you—ah—owe your very remarkable success. I may say you owe your good fortune chiefly to that—ah—to say the least of it peculiar, person, Mr. Draper of Unity. As you—ah—may be aware, I never agreed with Mr. Draper's views on certain aspects of Hellenic life and thought: I have indeed endeavoured to counteract his influence in my lectures. It appears—

ah—that your answer to a certain question in the general paper, doubtless set by Mr. Draper himself—ah—a libertine, of course, in every way, exactly met with Mr. Draper's own views. Ah—you doubtless know which question I refer to. I cannot decently discuss the matter with you now, but—ah—I feel it my duty as a minister of the Church as well as your tutor to give you a few words of advice in taking leave of you and wishing you a—ah—happier continuance of your success. I pray you may be delivered from the error of your ways—ah—by meeting as soon as possible with a good woman whom you may make your wife—ah."

Denis could not listen another moment to his sacrilegious drivel. He felt a wild impulse to shake the life out of the unhappy, stammering Mr. Monson; but all he dared trust himself to do was to shake the abject little man's shrivelled hand in silence, and with a conventional word of farewell to hurry from the room. He must go to Jim at once. How strange, how wonderful that the unlettered young working lad would be able to appreciate his success at its true value, while his official tutor could only as sit there gasping impious inanities and making himself thoroughly uncomfortable in the doing of it!

In three hours' time he was racing with feverish steps down one of the platforms of the Central Station at Middletown. Suddenly he paused and removed his hat. There was his hero and his good genius, the guiding inspiration of his success, busily hurling parcels into the luggage-van of the evening North express, unaware of his presence, almost on the very spot where Denis had first met him, but, as it seemed to him, more beautiful than ever, his face transfigured in the dim light of the van. As the last parcel was in and the whistle sounded for departure, Jim closed the door and turned to meet his friend's adoring gaze.

"Denis, good old mate," he cried. "So you have come back at last. And what about the examination?"

"Dear old Jim," Denis whispered as he clasped his beloved's work-roughened hand, "*you* have got the most brilliant first of the year."

"I don't know what you mean," replied the boy, evidently bewildered and obviously a little disconcerted by his friend's demonstrative bearing, for a large gentleman in an expansive ulster with several suit-cases and a case of golf-clubs was eyeing them with more than a little curiosity.

"Go now and relive that splendid type of the normal Briton of some of his bundles, and don't answer any of his questions for an extra three pence," returned Denis lightly; "I'll explain as we go home. You come off soon?"

"In ten minutes, at 8.30. Mrs. Birch will be surprised to see you."

"He doesn't understand," Denis mused, as the lad turned aside to attend the wants of the large gentleman with the bulky luggage; "but he shall—he must—realise how much I owe to him. Tonight we shall celebrate the bridal feast of our friendship."

For twenty minutes, as the strange pair walked through the crowded central streets, and later through the quiet suburban thoroughfares of the city, Denis tried to make Jim realise how vast an inspiration his love had given to his career. He felt a little disappointed with the progress of his explanation, for Jim, who always seemed to follow him at least with sympathy if not with the understanding of culture, appeared tonight to be paying scant attention.

"Well, old pal," Jim interpolated at last, a little impatiently, "I'm glad you have got through so well, though of course that's all rot what you say about me doing it for you. But I've a bit of news for you too, though I didn't put it in my letters, for—I didn't somehow quite know how you'd take it. As a matter of fact, I've got a young lady at last. She works in a jewellery factory— I'll show her to you tonight; I've arranged to meet her at the other end of Albert Road. I'm sure you'll like her, and we shan't be any worse mates because I'm walking out with a girl, shall we?"

These last words a little anxiously, for Jim had caught a glimpse of the pained look on Denis' face. They had reached the junction of several roads, at the opposite end of Albert Road from Jim's rendezvous.

Denis stood motionless, helpless, at the corner of the dull street. Something seemed to snap in his heart—the slender cord that he hoped had been enough to bind their two souls indissolubly together, even as the soul of David was knit with the soul of Jonathan. Then the moment for sacrifice had come, and he was powerless to avert it. Powerless, for he knew now that he was the sport of nature, while Jim was fulfilling the destiny of his normal healthy body and soul, and it would be sin as well as folly to raise a word of protest. But in the first pangs of his grief he saw, not his own renunciation, but the sacrifice of the beauty of his friend's glorious youth. He saw the ghastly vision of Jim the master of a workman's squalid tenement, surrounded by a blousy, slatternly wife and dirty snivelling children, the squalid discomfort of the single living room all around, and Jim himself the central figure—his beautiful, boyish face disfigured and coarsened, an ordinary, vulgar, unambitious toiler in the depths, middle-aged years before his time. Even now he seemed to notice for the first time a coarseness in Jim's tones, a banality in his expression, where before he had discerned nothing but the sparkle of youth and the sympathy of perfect friendship.

He dared not trust himself to speak many words. He stammered out some lame excuse that he was forced to meet a friend on business at the Station Hotel, and that he would have to go back there for the night.

"But you'll just come along and be introduced to my Lizzie!"

"No—go—you must not keep her waiting. I will write tomorrow."

He stood for a moment to watch Jim's eager, lovely, young figure speeding away down the poor street to meet his appointed fate, and to enjoy the brief romance of normal human love for which the wretched few equipped like himself, rich or poor, clever or stupid, virtuous or vicious, must substitute a life strewn with the wrecks of broken comradeships and shattered ideals, and suffer in silence in a world that denies their existence and will not brook to hear the truth. Then he turned away sorrowful.

He had reached the parting of the ways.

Barbara Marsham

I

BARBARA MARSHAM sat in her bedroom window looking out over the quiet landscape with a dissatisfied frown upon her handsome face. And yet in the remote silence of this late June evening the view was fair and peaceful enough to see. The dainty travelling-clock—a mere decorative trifle and nothing more—that stood upon the acajou writing-table with its silver-initialled pad of precise red morocco, its bright shining inkstand, pens, old candlesticks, seals, all in big apple-pie order, had just softly, almost as though fearing to interrupt, very softly chimed seven. A hazy mist, purple and indecisive like the bloom on a ripe plum, shrouded the coppice where sky and boscage touched, toning the velvet grass of intervening lawns with their long boundary lines of hedgerows to shadowed vagueness and neutrality. Beyond the silhouette tops of the trees the sun had set but a moment or two ago just where the broad sky flushed with a glory of orange, coquelicot, and gold that loitered long. A perfume of night-scented stock filled the air; Evening in her soft robes of hybrid mauby grey, the heavy lids drooping a little wearily over her dark eyes, stood at the gate.

In spite of the placid picture unfolding and glimmering before her, pervaded as it was with the calm melancholy of dusk and soothed by that solitude which swiftly falls while no human form is to be seen however lately man's tread has passed through the country lokes and lanes on his homeward way, Barbara showed active signs of intense irritation. Two deep lines furrowed across her high clean forehead, and discontent was rampant in the steady grey eyes beneath. Her mouth with its voluptuous lips, red and cruel, so striking in the pallor of a face which had hardly a touch of colour or warmth, was closed in the vice of a tight sullen obstinacy that few, if any, of her so-called intimate friends had ever suspected, far less ever seen. For Barbara, incontestably handsome, and often quite ungrudgingly termed beautiful even by women, though never pretty, studied her weak points more successfully than even her good features, and in so educative a process had long since thoroughly realised that at twenty-eight and more an uncurbed temper and annoyances too keenly resented are apt to stamp themselves in legible characters that defy both the most expensive Bond Street creams and the deftest touches of the slim-fingered masseuse wholly to erase.

Yet there were occasions—of late they had been rather frequent—when, especially in the privacy of her own room, she felt she must give vent to pure vexation or else be choked. The scheme of things was too foolishly muddled, too impossibly awry, and when she considered her past life in detail together with all the problems of the future as she had been somewhat minutely doing ever since tea-time that afternoon, she burned hot and cold with an anger beyond stoic control. She had indeed just made as frank and pitiless a self-examination as the most scrupulous devotee about to be shrived, and the result was bitterly to deplore the sins and shortcomings of the Powers, whatever they might be, who by their cynical jugglery of chance, luck, and circumstance had truly placed her for awhile in a pleasant position enough, but, when the draught drank sweetest, seemed with malice prepense to be about to dash the cup from her lips, and not to proffer any solace or compensation. She was increasingly conscious that as every year went by, almost every month now, her opportunity of gracefully extricating herself from a position of some insecurity grew less, her resistance to the trend of things necessarily more feeble and inept.

She wanted just to float with the stream. Nothing but a thoroughly comfortable life would ever suit her now. She knew and acknowledged that quite frankly and selfishly without the slightest attempt at veneer or disguise; and any tremor of romantic nonsense, even suppose such could ever venture to assault her calculating serenity must be firmly and immediately stifled. For, as she was in honesty bound to confess with regret and almost disdain,—(Barbara was perfectly open and merciless with herself despising those cotton-wool delicacies and adroit diplomacies with which the majority of us, even in the confessional box where we are both priest and penitent, are wont so tactfully to investigate our motives and intentions,)—once or twice at odd moments she had felt a galvanic thrill which momentarily unsettled her purpose just a little, and some thrust of emotion found, it would seem, a chink in the armour, showing that perhaps after all there was something worth questing beyond the mere flesh pots of Egypt. The memory of a picnic on the river when she had been little more than a girl, and the slim figure of a bare-throated young punter so clean in his spotless flannels, so unerring in the nice conduct of the long pole, rankled in her mind. She found it impossible too to banish as completely as she would wish the echo of a boyish laugh and the firm grasp of a lithe-limbed subaltern—a hopelessly ineligible *parti*—as in the early dawn they danced together the last of many waltzes.

Such thoughts at the present moment only chafed her irritation to an open sore, and she quite gratuitously began to accuse herself of weakness and sentimentality, which were in truth unbeknown traits in her character. Why talk of love when there's work to be done? The art of living,—of seeking that is to say an existence replete with all the material amenities and little pleasurable essentials that alone make life really tolerable—suddenly seemed to be about to entail a considerable amount of effort and no few distasteful activities.

Life at Elsenham, had she been married and her own mistress there, would have suited her very fairly well. A little dull perhaps at times, especially in the fall of the year, when the rack of autumn leaves lay in great mouldering heaps at the corners of the garden and bestrewed the dingle, when winter with its seasonable jollifications, skating, dances, Christmas theatricals, routs, hogmanays, had hardly begun; for Barbara did not shoot although occasionally she would motor out to lunch with the guns when there were house-parties at Cotham Park or the Rounthwaites. The fact is that unless she could find plenty to occupy her time, which plenty must be mainly done in the society of others, the country tended to bore her. It had not been so of course at first when her mother married Mr. Quartermaine, and they newly came to live at Elsenham twelve years ago. The countryside, the obvious opulence, the well-ordered house with its clique of trained servants, the absence of domestic worldly affairs, had seemed Paradise itself, but now she took all these things for granted, absolute necessities and everyday needs.

She simply could not bear to think of her life before she was sixteen. What it had been until her father died she did not well remember. Her only recollections were of a suburban villa in an intolerable side-street of suet-coloured houses, all of one ugly pattern two stories high, all separated from the noisy road that rang incessantly with the clutter of small tradesmen's carts, with bicycle bells and harsh shouts of errand boys, just by a few feet of narrow ochre gravel and a group of dusty shrubs that seemed petrified in their stunted misery. From the busy High Street, only a couple of hundred yards away, came the ceaseless hum of innumerable electric tram cars with the deeper bourdon of motor buses ploughing through the congested traffic. How she hated the tiny iron gates that grinned rustily and banged in monstrous succession all down the featureless row as the heavy-footed postman trudged from "Balmoral" to "The Acacias," from "The Acacias" to "Bon Repos". For sheer lack of occupation she had often stood at the dining-room window and watched his progress, idly speculating whether he would come to their own door or not, and feeling a stupid sense of disappointment when he passed by, although she rarely received a letter herself, and, so far as she knew, nothing he might bring could concern her for good in the slightest degree. Often for two and three days together their letter-box was empty save when a halfpenny circular or a meretricious sales catalogue fell in. How she had loathed the stuffy dining-room saturated with greasy smells of cooking and haunted by the ghosts of immemorial cold mutton meals. She could never forget the square table with its faded red serge cloth almost taking up all the available space, so that the three straight-backs and comfortless old rep sofa had to be pushed right against the walls on which they left dents and bad marks, crowding the wicker arm-chair and a little Victorian davenport into obscure corners. One of the dingy brown laths in the ill-fitting Venetians was badly broken—it was never repaired—and the light from the lamp-post opposite the gate used to stream in directly on to the supper table. All the ornaments on the mantle-piece were chipped. Nothing that was whole could be spared from the drawing-room, a minute back parlour, where Mrs. Marsham congregated the remnants that she had been able to secure from the general wreck at her husband's death in the hopes to make a brave little show. But year by year the rugs got shabbier, the furniture gloomier, the pictures sadder and more depressed. What an existence it was in that cramped up cubby with its dark passage of a hall, papered with marbly yellows, its steep narrow stairs, whose strip of carpet was suddenly metamorphosed to cocoa-nut matting, at the bend where the first flight turned and debouched on to a tiny landing furnished with a giant cistern that from time to time whenever the lavatory was used undisguisedly sent forth a Niagarean sound of swiftly rushing waters through the whole house. How stuffy the bedrooms were with their rattling casement-sashes and ill-joisted doors, always either too hot or too cold; how gritty the weed-grown garden squares overlooked at the side and fore by neighbouring windows and as often as not adorned with linen and cotton-lace curtains hung out to dry; how deplorable the untidy third-rate meals, the gimcrack furniture, cheap patterned lino, the dullness, the shabbiness, the shifts and the saving, the incessant bickering with a procession of impudent slatternly servants interluded with open warfare when at any sudden exit, drunk and out-spoken charwomen filled the temporary gap before the advent of a more reliable retainer. For a while Barbara only knew the discomforts of her home life during her holidays, for she had been educated at an unfashionable and remote boarding-school at Malvern Wells, presided over by the relict and sister of a local rector. Her only other change from the underworld of Suburbia had been an annual three weeks each September, when she was due to stay at Huntingdown with a great-aunt, Mrs. Hamilton, a

154

relative who (as the child suspected) largely if not entirely paying for her schooling was perhaps curious to see what return could be got from money laid out. This starch old dame of nearly fourscore, still preternaturally agile and disagreeable for her age, being morosely religious in a Calvinistic way, and given to much conventions, exacted unremitting attentions and frequent attendance at certain missionary *mêlées* and evangelical reunions, where prayer and tea, both equally weak and worthless, were plentifully disbursed. Night after night too she required the reading aloud with proper emphasis and precision of various select pamphlets which either gave lurid details of the geography of hell and quite remarkable statistics as to those who at the end of their mortal career might infallibly expect to become better acquainted with that locality, or else attacked with foul-mouthed rancour and a crude distortion and ignorance of practical and historic fact the Society of Jesus and the Sacrament of Penance. This three-week interval however was very grateful to Mrs. Marsham since it enabled her to close her house each year, and give her domestic, supposing she had one at the moment, a holiday, whilst she herself paid a brief visit, for which she saved and pinched eleven months of the twelve, to a northern Hydro.

This was her only pleasure, nay more, it was the one link which fastened her to the social circles whence her husband's death had summarily forced her. Lucas Marsham, a colonial product merchant, had openly lived at the rate of twelve hundred a year, and had died worth nothing. What he left already belonged to his creditors. A pretty taste in horse flesh and a pretty taste in whore's flesh, both unsuspected by his wife, was brought to light at his rather sudden demise, and only by superhuman exertions had Richard Marsham, J.P. of Westbury, county Bucks and the Rev Broadbent Marsham, reverend dean of Shippea, dioceses Ely, both men of the strictest morality and unimpeachable motives, succeeded in stifling what promised to be a very lively scandal. Not the least difficult person to deal with at this eye-opening and expensive juncture had been their sister-in-law. Showing the utmost disregard for the memory of her deceased husband, to whom indeed, on the one occasion when she spoke of him, she coldly alluded to as "an unprincipled libertine and double dealer," she had by no means proved docilely amenable to preventing talk "for the sake of the family," but had insisted upon, as the price of her tractability and the quiet swallowing of her wrongs, an annual maintenance. Genuinely shocked at such an attitude her two brothers-in-law, after some hesitation, upon the advice of their solicitor agreed, but in spite of her determination she was only able to secure little more than a pittance, for she was shrewd enough to see that if she held, as she was at first inclined to do, for a larger sum than they tendered they would wash their hands of the bargain and sit down pained but reproachless to the scandal. Unexpectedly too Mrs. Hamilton, on being apprised of the state of affairs,—a happy stroke this on the part of the Rev. Broadbent, which enabled him to suggest to his brother a smaller figure than would otherwise have been possible for the widow's income, "hush money" the magistrate had once called it in a fit of apoplectic passion,—had come forward and proffered to apply for the schooling of little Barbara, always provided that the child was sent to an academy of her own choosing, "conducted on the soundest Protestant principles." Mrs. Marsham, who to save herself trouble and expense would indifferently as far as religion went have consented that Barbara should be educated by a Shaman or a rain-wizard, gladly accepted. She then retired to a cheap and distant suburb, and set about the dismal work of making sixpence go as far as nine pence halfpenny, and of systematically laying by a little cash each month for her holiday. Those three weeks were her sheet anchor, a real emblem of hope. From one of these holidays she had emerged triumphant with the news of her engagement to Mr. Quartermaine.

Barbara's schooling, partial and prejudiced though it was, did not prove altogether quite so sterile as might well have been the case. A goodly bevy of girls, and amongst the many prigs a few rebels, had been collected together at Little Foley House. This number necessitated the employ of a stolid German governess, who being also acquainted with French and a fair pianist, was worked like a hack-horse for a microscopic wage. This accident however was the cause of Barbara, who since she was neither rebel nor prig had little to occupy her time save application, being well-grounded in two languages and gaining a certain mechanical precision in music, a foundation, which when later on after her mother's marriage she passed to a fashionable finishing school, was not without its value. Yet for all the good she got from it, at the time she was never able to make up her mind if term at Malvern Wells was not even worse than her suburban home. The clanging bell at six twenty-five, winter and summer, the prolonged prayers at seven, the hour's hungry 'prep' before a breakfast of clammy porridge and thick-set damp brown bread, the perpetual revolution of dull interminable lessons, the quotidian boiled rice and treacle or rhubarb jam, the meal at five-o'-clock—half past five on Sundays—of dripping toast and weak watery tea, pictureless dusty or mudded walks in a trudging crocodile, worship three times on the Sabbath with the severest psalmody and interminable sermons roared by a bellicose old fanatic in a Genevan gown and black kid gloves, week in, week out, aching fingers drumming on yellow keys to an accompaniment of pencil raps and carrion-breathed Teutonic interjections, the hoarse bass and nascent white chin-bristles of Mrs. Gannaway, the shiny nose and bleating pipe of Miss Matty—indelible memories of fifteen years ago!

Yes, life at Elsenham was pleasant after all; and Barbara looked round her room with some complacency. The highly polished mahogany, the dark soft carpet, the brass bed with its flowered chintz curtains, the easy chairs, the deep cushioned sofa, the capacious wardrobe with its levelled mirror reaching to the ground, the dressing-table covered with innumerable brushes, bottles, boxes and perfumes, the little bookcase and not too many books, the bright pictures which had a few years before successfully displaced the old engravings that used to hang on the walls, the very bowl of flowers, all spoke of taste, comfort, enjoyment. The past was gone like a frightful nightmare, best ignored and forgotten. This was the present. But how to insure the present, how to make it permanent and staple, that was the immediate question. Only a day or two ago, not for the first time, her mother had spoken a few apparently casual yet quite purposeful words reminding her that Neil Quartermaine would be twenty-one early next year. And Elsenham then came to him. Barbara knew that there was no question of an undiluted villa warren again, at least not such as of old, but if this boy, whom as a factor she had long since ceased to count and whose occasional presence she almost ignored, did really want Elsenham for himself, and at his majority proposed to turn them both out neck and crop it would mean—well, it would mean a considerable difference all round. And Barbara Marsham was not disposed to contemplate the possibility of any other styles of living, of nothing at any rate that would entail retrenchment and economy.

As she looked out over the garden the frown again goffered her forehead, and the blind tassel with which she had been mechanically playing dropped from her fingers. Elsenham was no lordly demesne, not a large estate by any manner of means, as estates go, still it was quite big enough. Of course if she were mistress absolute there would have to be a house or at least a Kensington flat in Town as well, to escape to when one was ennuyé, but that could be easily managed. And to think that next year it would pass opportunities and all to a silly scatter-headed boy, who this evening was coming down home from Oxford!

"Why, Barbara, you've not begun dressing yet, and it's well after half-past seven."

Mrs. Quartermaine standing at the doorway spoke in a tone of distinct reproof; and reproof administered by Mrs. Quartermaine had a faculty of conveying much more censure than precisely the same words and phrases uttered by anyone else. It was not altogether her voice or intonation, but a certain masterfulness of manner which always seemed the dominant note in her atmosphere. Opponents wilted before her, whilst the imperial despotism of her mere presence had been known effectively to gag even the most contrary and determined antagonists.

Barbara looked up languidly enough. "Dinner's not till a quarter past eight, is it?" she said, half leaning round, "I've got plenty of time to change."

"I hoped you would be down when Neil arrived."

"Oh, I can't bother about that tiresome boy. I'm not going to make any difference for him, I can tell you, mother. I only have to slip on my white tussore."

"I beg you'll do nothing of the sort, Barbara," Mrs. Quartermaine re-joined, a more decisive note sounding in her acid voice. "I beg you'll do nothing of the sort," she repeated, coming a little way into the room, and closing the door after her. "I'll send Millón to you at once. Wear the black chiffon. It suits you much better."

"So it may," replied Barbara, rather petulantly, "but I really don't see why you should make all this ridiculous fuss over Neil. What does it matter what I wear tonight?"

"You don't seem to realise even yet, you foolish girl," said her mother drawing nearer and speaking in a low but intenser tone, "that if we are to remain on here at Elsenham you'll have to marry Neil Quartermaine."

The buzz and drone of a motor were heard outside.

"There he is. Don't be late."

Instead of booking to Framley which would have meant an awkward change and a wait to catch the little slow side train to Framley and Hanersh station, a miserable dilatory performance, Neil Quartermaine preferred to run down to Guildford by the 6.15 and thence drive to Elsenham Priory. Accordingly he had wired that morning directing the car to meet him at the White Hart, High Street, at 7.30 sharp. It must be confessed that he felt just a little bit daring when he wrote out his telegram; it was the first time that he had ventured to summon the motor without duly writing, if not exactly to ask the permission, at least to consult the convenience, of his step-mother, and had he wanted to ask it a year or two ago he felt pretty certain that some very patent excuse would have been found to say No. Upon the receipt of a letter three or four days ahead it had been arranged on the last two occasions at any rate, that he should be comfortably met at Guildford, but at the same time he was more or less clearly given to understand that this was in the nature of a favour and a concession. Neil, however, had begun to realise a little more practically of late that in rather under a year now not only the cars, but Elsenham itself, house, acres and all, would be his own with no one to control, to consent, or to say him nay.

Soon after the train raced through the many-platformed Clapham Junction Neil tossed aside the couple of evening papers he had bought at the Waterloo bookstall, and leaning his back against the well-padded cushions gave himself up to thought aided by a Turkish cigarette. There was no intruder in the first class carriage he had somewhat carefully chosen, for the train was pretty full, and as it dashed along with growing speed he felt himself free to meditate without fear of interruption.

First, there was his attitude at home.

This would need a good deal of care. Neil had not as yet definitely settled details of action even in his own mind, but he was face to face with the fact that in order to gain his chief end he must at once initiate a campaign, in which the sending of his telegram without a premonitory letter, was move number one, the first pawn. It was not until some six months before, in January last, when he had been a guest up in Yorkshire at the coming of age of his Wadham chum, Archie Fothergill, and seen behind the gay social curtain the flood of business which had suddenly overwhelmed poor Archie, the interviews with the family solicitor, with the local firm of lawyers, with the executors, with the steward, and the multitudinous parchments which had to be overlooked, the minutia it became essential to understand, the seemingly chaotic provisions which needs must be explained, a long tale nightly poured into his ears by the pyjama-clad figure of his friend, incessantly jibbing and caprioling under the whole loathed business with much self-pity and plaint, that Neil himself realised with something like a shock that in less than another year's time, when he too came to be twenty-one, he would be caught up helplessly and put through the ponderous mill of affairs. Of course Elsenham was small in comparison with the Fothergill estates, but yet it would bring ample responsibility and ownership for Neil to contemplate with any degree of equanimity.

There often lie far down in our minds determinative modes of action, fully planned and detailed, though not even framed in our conscious thoughts nor appreciated by our judgement, which when certain happenings occur, flash into being like the spark that jets from the flint struck with steel, and which we follow instinctively and deliberately, in obedience to an innate logic that, although unexpected and perhaps inexpressible in words, is none the less then infallibly our guide and counsellor. And so how often are deeds done or speeches spoken "on the spur of the moment," as the phrase goes, nothing but the inevitable outcome of systematic action, each separate factor of which may appear unrelated, or of a passive course of thought, which, given the juxtaposition of various circumstances, must perforce result in an event that, although it may seem strange and unreal to those who have not been able to delve below the surface and to discover the latent forces and protracted play of emotion beneath, is psychologically and substantially deducible from what went before. A mind that is single and severely logical may nearly always attain its end. The mind of youth is single but seldom logical at all. The mind of mature years is often scrupulously logical, but rarely single, being diverted into and filtered by a thousand interests that in destroying unity splinter concentration. It needs some red-hot passion, some vast ambition, some hate or love, to weld and sustain the two qualities in one strenuous and enduring force, unmalleable by environment.

As soon as Neil seriously began to review the dawning situation he very promptly and firmly made up his mind upon one point. The fact is that almost unknown to himself and certainly unformulated in his conscious thought his decision had been arrived at years before. When he attained his majority Mrs. Quartermaine and Barbara could no longer have their home at Elsenham. He would be very loath to treat them in a way that might savour of unkindness or injustice, so shrank somewhat from too premature a pronouncement of his future plans, lest such might be overtly suspected of indecent haste, and yet at the same time he could but realise that the sooner they were well aware of his resolve the better. Go they must. Much as he would have liked to have done so, he did not disguise from himself moreover that he was bound to encounter no little difficulty in the process of shifting his step-mother from the house she had gained by the one weapon of wit, with everything against her, time, equipment, resources, and had so long and so adequately swayed supreme, first dominating, without ever letting one crack of the whip be heard, a fractious and hypochondriacal husband, then after his death ruling unquestioned in her own right with cold justice and perfect serenity. Neil vaguely began to sketch out a mode of apprising her of his intentions: he sometimes pictured the many possible situations, and even once or twice had got so far as to rehearse scenes and dramatic dialogue, himself calmly insistent and firm, Mrs. Quartermaine argumentative and pleading. He consistently, however, set the stage for the climax in act four, quite neglected acts one, two and three. Dryden, it is said, used to curse the inventor of fifth acts: Neil Quartermaine's difficulty was with the exposition, the anagnorisis seemed simplicity itself. No doubt there must be a tussle, and some days of feverish happenings, which it might perhaps be cowardly to avoid by absence. Yet, was not that a possible, and even the more graceful course? If he were to spend the following Easter in Paris or Spain the two outgoers would at least feel that they were unwatched in their departure.

After all, he was sure of his ground, and it only meant sticking to his guns. He knew that Elsenham was his without embarrassment or deduction of any kind, save that—and he was heartily glad of the proviso—his father's will made ample allowance for Mrs. Quartermaine in the shape of an income sufficiently comfortable to relieve her from any anxiety as to the future, and himself from the slightest ghost of a feeling that he was in any way condemning her and Barbara to genteel difficulties.

Mr. Meriton too would back him up. Meriton had never liked Mrs. Quartermaine. He was a sure ally was old Meriton, the lean, frosty, meticulous saturnist, whom Neil almost always pictured as he could remember seeing him years ago when he used to go down to dessert for ten minutes before bed-time, and was perched on too high a chair at the table with its spotless napery and gleaming silver, a little lad eating nuts or almonds and raisins and looking up with awe and curiosity at the tall figure opposite him with its vast expanse of white shirt front, an ogre that gently fondled a glass of port in one bony hand and in the other clasped a fragrant cigar with the most delicate reverence for the gradual growth of grey ash. Neil used to be rather afraid of the oak-panelled dining-room. He did not so much mind going down in summer, but in winter when the room was all shadows save just the soft circle of light cast by the red-shaded candles, there was no knowing what might be hiding in the dark corners or who might suddenly step through some secret door in the wall, especially if you had been reading *Rookwood* or *Old London Bridge* half an hour ago, and then coming back again you had to run upstairs pretty quickly in case Herne the hunter with his antlers and rusty chain or the sailor who said he was Apollyon and who waited for little boys might be hiding at the end of one of the corridors.

Neil found something formidable about Mr. Meriton even now. Recently, in April last, when he had paid a private visit to the offices of Meriton and Pruet—(who Pruet was nobody could tell and so far as human knowledge went he had never been seen of mortal man)—in Lincoln's Inn Fields, in order to make doubly sure that his father's will did not contain any conditions or codicil with reference to Elsenham which would hamper and restrict his future plans, he had not felt altogether at ease under the scrutiny of the beady eyes staring from beneath bushy unkempt brows. Yet when he was being ushered into the frowsty back office he had told himself for the thousandth time that he was only going to see an elderly man with a very sound but by no means great reputation as a lawyer, a nice taste in intaglios, and a digestion. He had got the information he wanted, cut and dry, and although reassured, he had ventured on a hint that when his majority came he purported to make considerable changes at Elsenham, not a flicker of light in the dull abstract gaze, not a muscle moving in the yellow mask-like face gave the slightest indication of interest or of a desire to know more of his future plans. But Neil was very well aware that for the past eleven years Mr. Meriton's visits to Elsenham had been far briefer and less frequent than in the olden days, and during the four and a half years since Roger Quartermain's death the lawyer, who had been left a trustee of the estate and a co-guardian of the boy, had only run down for a few hours at a time, never sleeping and seldom taking a meal in the house. Mr. Meriton quite extraordinarily disliked the handsome masterly widow who by her little feminine slight of flattery and cockering had so successfully hooked his whimsical old friend at the Buxton hydro. Most of the necessary business to be transacted from time to time was done by correspondence as bloodless and formal on the one side as on the other. With regards to Neil there had been really nothing to settle. His career was already clearly defined for the next few years. When he left Uppingham he was to go to Univ, and everything had smoothly eventuated along the given lines without hitch or jar. The last year or two Neil had been at Elsenham for the greater part of his various holidays and vacations was spent with his own chums, abroad once or twice, in Brittany, in Florence, in Rome, with reading parties or on visits. In spite of some anaemic suggestions from his step-mother he never asked anyone to stay at the Priory. That would come later. But he had several times had his friends down to Cornish fishing-villages and on Devon moors as his guests.

Although he had never known his mother—she had died after a hard labour in giving him birth—Neil secretly, but yet not a whit the less bitterly, resented the intrusion of another in her place, the entry of a petticoat where for nine years petticoat had never ruled. It was quite an illogical dislike, and therefore all the more certain to be deeply rooted in his mind, When an individual is capable of calmly analysing his antipathy to another, of estimating and weighing exactly what quality or the lack of what quality, spiritual, mental, physical, is it that annoys and repels him, then with a little pinch of philosophy in the nostrils from the snuff box of common-sense, a little bird's eye view perhaps of his own short-comings, he may soon well be able to take his bête noire to his bosom. But when it is a case of *Non Amo te, Sabidi*, then all the reason and common-sense in the world won't run to a candid head-shake. Natural instances are more grounded in mankind than logic.

Neil really shunned Mrs. Quartermaine as much as Meriton himself did. And as he sat in a carriage on the London and South Western, hurrying towards Guildford he began to realise even more fully what a strong aversion he had for his step-mother. It was not a question of any positive quality which she might possess or express, although indubitably she was a very positive person, it was something beyond that, some trait deep down in the grain of her individuality which seemed to irk and rile him to uncontrollable impatience. She was to him like a harsh blend of colours, a discord in music, which grate and fill the atmosphere with uneasy fretful waves of ether.

Certainly he could not contemplate spending very long at Elsenham with Mrs. Quartermaine everlasting-ly in evidence. But perhaps she would be going away for July; she often did. Then he might as well make a start and have someone down for a week or two, Jack Bellinger, or Runciman, or Archie. It would all help to break the ice a bit and point the way to what was coming next year. At the same time though before he went up again he ought to let them quite unmistakably see that she should expect them to make a move in the spring, by Easter at the latest. He supposed they would have to get a house somewhere . . . Houses are easily enough got, and Barbara was always grousing about the country being dull. Well, here was a chance for her. Her mother could take a flat in Town, they could cram it with people morning, noon and night, all night too as far as he cared, and be happy . . . yet there was no getting away from the fact that it was going to be a damned nuisance having to tell Mrs. Quartermaine to quit, and no doubt he must look forward to a thick time of it until they had cleared out, bag and baggage, for good and all.

His thoughts became so busy that when the train drew-up in Guildford station he was for a moment bewildered and could hardly believe they had already arrived. Papers were abandoned unread; kit-bags and portmanteau, rescued from the pile of luggage that was being swiftly vomited out on to the platform, were consigned to a porter with directions to bring them up to the White Hart straightaway.

As Neil strolled slowly up to the slope of the High Street he found the sleepy old town inexpressibly soothing and grateful. In the warm russet light of an early summer evening tiers of quaint roofs and the tower of St. Michael's stood sharply defined against the clear sky. The White Hart itself looked fresh and saintly with its overhanging balconies and window-boxes of scarlet geraniums and white moon-daisies, just a little bit too much like a set scene on the boards perhaps, but still quite countrified notwithstanding a patent touch here and there, a garage sign, a bright motoring notice, to show that they were thoroughly up to date and modern for all the unsophisticated rusticity.

Outside stood the car waiting right enough, and with a nod and a word or two for Haines, the clean-shaven young chauffeur, who stood almost as if to attention, Neil passed up the stone steps into the quaint old-fashioned snuggery of a smoke-room bar at the end of the black beamed passage. As he drank his gin and angostura it pleased him to look round the fresh smart little place so beautifully kept with its elaborate simplicities, the gay flowers in thick blue china bowls, the dark oak polished till it shone like a mirror, the chairs which might well have been real antiques, the leaded casement and soft-cushioned window seat, the valanced chintzy curtains, the shining pewter and glass, all tending to create just the right impression of solid eighteenth-century comfort and peace. It was all so very well done that instead of the elegantly-coiffured and gay-bloused young lady opposite him it only needed Cherry or Gipsy in a mob and dimity justicore to be a set for *The Beaux' Stratagem*.

A few minutes later he was in the car, which, under the superb pilotage of Haines, glided with swift unerring ease down the incline, over the bridge, towards the open country beyond.

Neil felt indescribably satisfied as he neared his home.

Elsenham Priory was a large building, ante-Tudor in the main, close to the road, but separated from it by a broad expanse of lawn, the boundary of which, an old stone wall of moderate height pierced by heavy wrought-iron gates, was further topped by a tall fringe of thick trees completely screening all external observation, save for a tantalising peep that could just be obtained through the iron-scrolled arabesques. The house consisted of a long low block, more deep than high, mellowed with age, to which had been added in the reign of Mary or Elizabeth two shortened wings, the whole forming three sides of a rectangle. These enclosed a shallow gravelled court on to which debouched the broad drive whilst to the right lay the terraced gardens and parterres, fragrant with flowers. Behind extended slightly more modern premises, domestic offices screened off with ivied walls and hedgerows that led by red-tiled paths and pergolas to a great kitchen garden, orchards, meadow lands and woods.

The shadows were falling swiftly now, but lights had not yet begun to twinkle through the long rows of windows, diamond-paned and deep-silled, whence had faded but a few minutes before the roseate flush of sunset. It was all very still. Hardly a breath seemed to be stirring in the country lanes, and the one thin thread of smoke that escaped from the tall twisted chimney-stacks rose up straight unwavering into the clear air. The cawing of the rooks, as they made their way in a dark squadron to the further coppice, was the only sound that broke the silence.

Neil looked upon his inheritance and saw that it was very good.

II

The morning sun shone brightly through a chink in the window curtains where they just did not meet, and fell full on the face of the sleeping boy.

It was a pleasant ample room into which the golden light penetrated so fresh and cleanly.

The walls, covered with a paper like old-fashioned chintz, had only a few antique engravings hanging upon them, but over the mantelpiece were two or three Sicilian studies and an excellent reproduction of a well-known Tuke. An easy chair spoke of capacious lounging comfort, and a genuine gate-legged table had its writing materials, silver-framed photographs, and in the centre a dragon blue bowl of crimson and creamy roses. A carved dwarf bookcase overflowing with books and papers occupied one corner, but for the rest there appeared the usual bedroom properties, the long row of boots in their little polished shelf, the tall-boy of dark mahogany, the chintzy ware upon the washstand, the bath-gown behind the door.

The sun duly attracted by the dressing-table glittered and sparkled amongst the silver, glass and steel spread out over the immaculate damask toilet. For some minutes it had not spared to concentrate itself upon the figure in the bed, the crisp curly hair, the strong white throat and naked chest where the collar of the mauve pyjama jacket had been left unbuttoned and free.

Neil moved his tousled head once or twice on the pillow, grunted, then slowly opened his eyes. Half asleep and blinking he lazily waved one hand backwards and forwards as if to drive off a troublesome fly, then realising it was the sunshine not a midge or a moth, he rolled over and buried his nose amongst the bedclothes. It was useless however. A tiresomely elusive tickling sensation began to worry him. He kicked his legs out to their full length in the bed. His elbow itched, and as soon as he had rubbed it, his back felt mildly uncomfortable. His toes caught the crumpled sheet. At last in sheer despair he sat up, yawned lustily and stretched his arms. Upon a little table at his side lay his watch and seals. He put out a hand, and lifting it glanced at the time. Not quite seven-o'-clock! He yawned once more, and remembered it was Sunday morning. Even the servants would hardly be about. Perhaps the best thing to do would be to doze again for a bit. But that was impossible with the sun staring right on to the bed. He must see himself each evening that the curtains were drawn right across. The maid, or whoever it was, might have been more careful.

Slowly Neil threw back the clothes, and getting out of bed, crossed the room, walking delicately like Agag, to close up the traitorous little chink that had let the sunrays through, but as his hand was groping the chintz he realised he didn't want to go doze or sleep any more, and with a quick gesture pulled it back letting in a flood of golden light. The blind flew up in a moment, and he leaned out, breathing in the pure fragrant air, the beauty of the morning.

The English landscape was lovely indeed . . .

He had never endured a Maytime descent, like that of the Assyrian, of a female bevy to be superimposed upon long-suffering chums, to be billeted for tea at Magdalen or Trinity, and escorted daily to the riverside, night to College balls.

Questions and answers, such as they were, had ceased. Just the right amount too had been said about the happenings of the last three months at Elsenham. The gardens, it appeared, were exceptionally prolific in flowers. There had been a little trouble with one of the tenants on the estate, but that was all got over some time ago; in any case it was hardly worth mentioning now, certainly not worth discussing: Tollen thought the fruit would be unusually fine this season, the cherries were ripening quickly and the orchards promised to be early. Had it been warm at Oxford? Good weather for the rowing, for the . . . the . . . ? Eights; yes, of course, Eights. The canon had been poorly, very poorly, in fact he hadn't been in church for two Sundays. But that was a fortnight or more ago. A touch of bronchitis, and then he was so old. Why, he must be close on eighty. And of course the beginnings of May had been treacherous. But with the warmer weather he had picked up again wonderfully. Yes, his garden was looking beautiful. There was a new curate. Mr. Heneage—quite young; that is well under thirty at any rate. An Oxford man. Whatever college did he say he was at . . . King's or Balliol. Oh, wasn't there a King's? Surely there was something that began with a K. Keble? yes, of course, Keble. That was the name. Undoubtedly it was far better from every point of view to have a permanent man than these Saturday to Monday guinea-pigs. For one thing it almost entirely relieved the canon. Besides a resident curate could enter thoroughly into the life of the village . . . .

As the aimless talk trickled on, tasteless and fluid as water, Neil got more and more impatient. He fidgeted, missed his cues, and failed to ask the obvious questions. It was all so useless and so boring. And this he realised with a mental shudder was only the first of many nights. When one dries up after an hour a visit of several weeks is a melancholy prospectus.

It was not until just before the appearance of the sweets that a decent silence was permitted, and that only because Mrs. Quartermaine had for the moment exhausted her artillery of small gossip. It was an effort to keep it up indefinitely unless her listeners supplied fuel by some faint indication of interest; an ejaculation, perfectly inept in itself, a desultory murmur of half-heard words, even a polite gesture of assent, any of these would have been sufficient. Really when she tried to make conversation it was only fair that others should take their part. Otherwise it tended to become a rather monotonous soliloquy. She was even at her best when confronted with some show of resistance that moved her to the task. Passivism blunted her weapons. She thought Neil was very stupid this evening, stupider than usual, and almost boorishly inattentive. Words had had to be dragged out of him. She looked round the table rather vexedly.

Barbara, who had been eating with fastidious nicety as her wont, was dipping her well-manicured nails into the silver bowl at her side, whilst Neil, his eyes on his plate, snowed white sugar over a scarlet pile of strawberries with an intense precision that would not have been improper in a chemical experiment.

"I suppose we shall have to ask him to dinner once at any rate while you are home. But I don't think it need be for a week or two yet."

Nobody answered.

Mrs. Quartermaine spoke again in a rather louder voice which vibrated with irritation. She wished Barbara would not be so *distraite*.

"I suppose we shall have to ask Mr. Heneage to dinner one evening!"

Neil looked up quietly. "Mr. Heneage?" he queried.

"Yes. The new curate."

"Oh. Why?"

"Well, it would only be the proper thing to do, I take it, now you are home. He's called twice. The first time we were out. Of course we shall all have to wake up and keep more or less in touch with the Church since there's new blood in the village. Besides, he's Oxford," she concluded vaguely.

"Please don't ask him on my account," said Neil rather coldly. "I really don't want to meet any parsons."

Mrs. Quartermaine frowned. "I think you'll find he's altogether different to the ordinary run of clergy. He's quite educated, and he's travelled abroad, in Switzerland, I believe, and Miss Peckering says he's going to do wonders here. I thought the Bellingers were rather churchy people."

"Churchy? Oh, perhaps Jack is, but hardly in the way which would suit the Canon and Hanersh, or Mr. Heneage either, I expect." And Neil smiled as he thought of Jack with his guilds and confraternities, his love of ceremonial and his ritual lore, in scope and accuracy rivalling Baldeschi or Monsignor Wallace; his encyclopaedic knowledge of the various Orders, monks, friars, hermits, clerks regular, congregations, nuns, sisters, beguines, tertiaries, oblates, Knight military, chevaliers, brown, black, white, blue, pied; his researches into Coronelli, Antonio de Yepes, Helyot, Bérengier, into hagiographies, menologies, and chronicles innumerable, the Bollandists, Ribadeneira, the Oratorian lives, the Monza Collana, abbé Duras, Marchese, the Franciscan Leon, Molano, and a score beside; his cult of some dilatus, such a patron as Sir John Schorne, "gentleman born," Henry VI, Thomas of Lancaster, his enthusiasm for the Venetian Marina, for the little shepherdess Pastorella, whose life Pallico has sweetly written, for the infant Simon of Trent; his devotion to the latest beato or servo di Dio, or even in jealous anticipation of Roman decrees, his rashly blazing the aureole around the heads of Benedetto Odescalchi and Canon Cottolengo, of Père Seurin, S.J. and Sor Patrocinio. Yet Jack Bellinger was a sound scholar, and, what is more, underlying all there ran a deep vein of the golden ore of mysticism. Only last night they had said Compline together in the dressing-room oratory with its little Neapolitan altar, decked with the musky frontal bought at some old shop in an Italian back street and the artificial flowers straight from Romanini's. Jack lit two candles—blue of course—at the Salve Regina.

"It all comes to the same thing in the end anyhow," remarked Mrs. Quartermaine comfortably.

"Judging by his sermons I don't think anyone could find Mr. Heneage particularly interesting, unless perhaps it's Hannah Pickering," said Barbara speaking almost for the first time.

Her mother cast a rebuking glance in her direction. "We have to do plenty of things and to know plenty of people who perhaps aren't particularly interesting," she replied in a rather acid voice.

"I really don't see why on earth we should," commented Neil meditatively. "Up at Oxford, if even I come across a man whom I find heavy and dull, I give him a wide birth, that's all. What's to be got from hob-a-nobbing with a lot of bores?"

"There are such things as social responsibilities," returned the lady.

"Oh, I suppose bores may have their drawing-room uses, though I confess even so I cannot quite see what these may be. 'To stop a hole to keep wind the away,' conversationally, I mean."

"I'm afraid your allusions and quotations are rather too clever for me".

". . .would hardly notice tomorrow morning even if half-a-dozen pipes or cigars had been going in here for hours."

And Neil struck a match.

"I am afraid that in spite of your magic water we should infallibly notice it in here when we aren't accustomed to smoke. Wouldn't it be pleasant to take your cigarette out on to the terrace?"

"Oh, I am sorry. I didn't see you hadn't finished." The match dropped into the finger-bowl with a quirk spurt and a tiny trail of blue smoke.

Mrs. Quartermaine rose. The boy was persistent. It was stupid, but hardly worth an argument; not at the moment at any rate.

"When you've had coffee perhaps you'd like a game of billiards. Barbara shall play you."

"Thanks," answered Neil, holding wide the door. "If I feel like a game I'll come across to the drawing-room and tell you."

"Say in about twenty minutes. I shall be busy then for I've some letters I must get written tonight," and she swept out followed in silence by her daughter.

Neil sighed rather audibly, and lighting his cigarette strolled across to the open window. He sank down on a broad cushioned sill and gazed meditatively at the dark landscape under the purpling sky in which hung a thin bow of gold.

I Shall in Two Minutes

"I shall in two minutes."

"Cuthbert, you will outstrip your master. I may as well introduce myself—Wilfrid Benedict Stanislaus etcetera and a lot more—Hogarth, at your service."

"And I'm only Cuthbert Annice Browns."

"If that spells you, it's quite enough.'

"I almost feel," said the boy, "that you will be more to me than I am to myself."

"Life is very sterile save we regard it in relation to others. How true it is that one does not really live one's own life, others live it for one. There is nothing, I sometimes think, in the whole world I would not give to go through my past again, to relive my youth. And yet even if my wish could be literally granted I know I should commit the same follies, fall into the same faults. Else it would not be worth the living. After all, experience is the name we give our mistakes. Yet in some way I shall be enabled to recapture the hours that have flown. I shall live through you. And to live through another is to experience every pleasure but no regret. To borrow another's life and to use it as one's own is a wonderful—a tremendous thing. That is what makes the art of the actor so fascinating. In their foolish way people often blindly ask why it is the stage is attractive to youth, and they talk meaningless nonsense about the glamour of the footlights. It allures simply because it is not glamorous, because it is reality: momentary and incidental maybe but none the less intense for all its transitoriness. We cannot measure feeling by mere duration. The pang of a minute often proves more poignant than the anguish of an hour. Length is not depth. The great actor as he treads the boards believes for the time in everything. The joy of Wildair is his joy, the tragedy of Castlio his own despair. The painted scenes are truer far than nature's landscapes or lawns. And so when life is young and full it seeks to capture every emotion, to pour itself out in the love of Romeo, in Hamlet's melancholy, to win for itself the careless wit of Dorimant, to make the intrigue of Dick Amlet its own. And those who when put to the test are unable to realise this, who are unable to sit on a throne with kings, to wallow in the gutter with a harlot, fail hopelessly, miserably mediocre as they are in their sterile renunciations. I would send my soul to track out every way, to taste every mood. For me no book is sealed. Let a man debauch nightly with rakes and Cyprians in vile houses of lust and shame, let him glut each sense to cloying with all the unearned luxury indulgence knows, or let him in some Gothic cloister sup all alone on lentils and cold water disciplining his body from dusk till dawn, yet if he be merely a spectator of the play and insincerity mother his sin as well as his virtue, how empty it all must be! So we are none the cleaner of our fasts and penances, none the wickeder for our vices and corruption. With us they are simply moods of the moment, each intensely precious for its own ephemeral loveliness, but as a permanent factor in our personality—no!"

He ceased, as the lad, who had been listening intensely, sipped his hock in silence for a minute or two with a puzzled air.

"Your philosophy is strangely enticing if one could only live up to it," he said at last.

"Why should we not? It is merely a question of courage."

"Then life is a series of moods?"

"Does not nature herself set us that example? This morning not long since she wore a veil of misty grey awhile; the trees are the colour of an autumn sunset. In a month or two they will be bare. The rime will cover them with its chill white runes when winter clasps them close in her icy fingers. The countryside will be shrouded in snow, and the moon hang blood-red in a clear sky. Then again as the pulse of youth beats quicker modest violets will peep out from the hedgerows and bluebells, and as the air grows warmer the breeze will be sweet with the perfume of fresh garden flowers. The murmur of stock-doves is heard in farm cotes. The iris will be purple and the lily silver as they were six months ago. It is only we alas! who cannot repeat our secrets and our experiences. Memory haunts us like a ghost that refuses to be laid, and we are sad for the opportunities we let go by, for the sins we were too cowardly to commit. One should never be afraid to open any door. Heaven may lie behind it."

"Suppose it hid some monstrous thing?"

"Then it should be shut again instantly. But even so probably it might afford an unforgettable moment—a new thrill, shall we say? There must be black to blend with colour. Could there be anything more exquisite than the dark cypress against the vivid azure of Italian skies? Their saturnine grace enhances all the sunlight and the blues. Literature were banal indeed without *Le Fleurs de Mal* and the satanic reveries of Edgar Poe. Baudelaire's only mistake was when he admitted Americans to hell."

"So we are to yield to the mood of the moment—"

"That is the wisest way."

"But does one not often regret——"

"One often regrets everything. And still if we are always true to the first elements of beauty, I think we need have no more regret for the drama of our own lives than the gentle pathos and sorrow we feel for the actors in some old Grecian tragedy, for Polyxena at the funeral pyre whilst the Argive youth with trembling hands and averted face shuddering hold the golden-pommelled sword to her snowy bosom, or for the blind old King of Thebes when he enters the mystic woods of the Dread Ladies and amid the solemn stillness that ever broods over that hallowed ground meets death with calm resignation and an awe that is not fear, or Antigone, in spite of edict and unjust laws, going out to scatter dust over her dead that lie unburied on the wind-swept plain."

"Yet does not life sometimes wound you?"

"Perhaps; but the scars soon disappear. Only the burnt child knows how delightfully warm the fire is. One must experience everything. You will find that life has exquisite emotions in store for you, feelings whose mere possibility you have never even guessed. You are young, oh how truly has it been said youth is the one thing worth having. So I who have lost it am bound to possess thro' another and live through you. Human life is but a mingled mass of pleasure and pain. And the same man must play many discordant parts. Our tragedies are merely farces with the laughter left out. They may be all the funnier."

He was aware as he talked that he had opened for the boy a new world, new ideas, and he felt like Diaz or Vasco da Gama when they first set their feet upon the yellow sands of some unknown shore in Mozambique. Only they were merely pioneers of a continent, he was the explorer of a living soul. Cuthbert watched him with large excited eyes, his lips were slightly parted, and his cheeks burned hectic red.

The soul is more interesting than a hemisphere. It has mysteries to reveal and deserts to traverse far more impenetrable than the Aztec forests or the limitless tracts of Sahara. To surrender oneself to life and all the potentialities of life without a struggle, without remorse, that seems indeed to some the highest ideal. Yet it is a philosophy which will brook nothing save the most complete self-abandonment; the man who refrains is a failure. It is only those who do not know life as it really is—life with all the intensity of its sensations be they even black and macabre or exotic or perverse,—that dare to deny, and starve their bloodless bodies of the fruit of the garden. The very horror of the shadows often makes the golden light richer and more rare. The curiosity about life is a thing which ever grows and is never satisfied.

The surgeon for all his scalpel and raspatory, carving the white body and tearing it into shreds, blanching each vertebra and bone, is impotent to discover those cells—are they in the brain or the blood?—which hold the origin of life. The scientist with all his jargon of sesquipedalian words, his library and intellect, is brought face to face with a breachless barrier. And, after all, can knowledge add fragrance to the rose or make a Maytide morning one whit lovelier?

As he looked at the lad opposite him he felt that he had in somewise recaptured to a certain extent at least his youth. Himself he was too often listless and tired, yet there was much to be done if one only had the energy and the instruments. There were pleasures to renew, sorrows to avenge. By means of another he could strike more subtly and more surely; through this boy, so dimly conscious of his own possibilities, he would once again taste of things he felt were fast slipping away.

"You are explaining a great deal to me," Cuthbert said, "but it is difficult to grasp it all at once."

"My lesson takes a life-time to learn," murdered the other.

The citron light which had almost already begun to fade a little, seemed to creep into each wineglass and stirred up the heart of the clear yellow hock until it

186

looked like liquid drops of amber and gold. The boy, who had just finished eating a peach, pushed away the plate a little and daintily dipped his fingers in the Cairene copper bowl. He did it with that intense attention we pay to trivial things whilst we are engaged in thinking of some important subject.

What a wonderful being he was, this boy, whom he had plucked from the rubble of the streets, nay, from death itself. Public School—the best product that England had given the world. Beauty too was his, a grace, such as rarely falls to the lot of British boyhood. Surely there was some strain of hot Southern blood, some near ancestor of Italy or the Peninsula.

Already he dominated him entirely and he could do anything with him he liked. It is a strange . . . a terrible possession—another human soul. It almost seemed like holding the prerogative of God Almighty Himself. Could any man imagine or desire a more fearful purchase? He smiled to himself as he thought of all that lay before him. No craftsman could boast such a tool as his. Cuthbert Brown would be to him a mirror in which he could see himself, feature for feature, and more than himself; himself in his youth but with undreamed of opportunities, more than money was able to buy. And he, as was fabled of mediaeval sorcerers, would project his soul into this lithe joyous body of nineteen years, would instil his desires, his passions into the boyish frame and make it vibrate in union with the workings of his brain, so eager to plan but sluggish to fulfil. The lad would show him his own soul more surely than any hours of morbid introspection or agony of repentance can reveal to a fanatic monk or a friar that lean and hungry psychology, which they so lust to know . . .

"You talk of moods," the boy cried petulantly, "is everything a mood then? What of love?"

"Ah, love is the mood that lasts."

There was silence for a moment.

"And here is Veney to tell us the motor is at the door. Work is about to begin."

Ghostly Godstow

This is the many-tentacled town,
This is the flaming octopus,
The ossuary of all of us.
At the country's end she waits,
Feeling towards the old estates.

SO wrote—or might we not truly enough say—so prophesied the Belgian poet Émile Verhaeren forty years ago. And in England even our Oxford—city of moony silence and tall sleeping spires—has awakened from her age-long dreams and flung out her arms on every side. The queen of English cities, proud, reticent, beautiful, has become a common harlotry. Her mystic charms she can never wholly lose. But ah! memory, however sweet, is bitter for those who remember her as once she was. Her very soul is smirched. Her sons, who once loved poetry, are now mad for politics.

There was no pleasanter walk of a summer afternoon than to take the towing path by the upper river, where on the farther bank the green expanse of Port Meadow stretches to the horizon, passing Bisney Church which lies back up a road "leading nowhere" as the village folk say, and so to Godstow with its ancient bridge, its tree-shaded ruins and the famous Trout Inn where undergraduates hum and swarm at tea-time and grumble and curse the English law which won't allow anything but soft drinks till six-o'-clock.

The old inn itself was part of the nunnery buildings—the guest-house in fact, where for eight centuries hospitality was dispensed to wayfarers from near and far. There is pitifully little left today of the great Benedictine Nunnery of Godstow. It lies across the river, opposite the Trout, and stands on an island formed by two small branches of the Thames. The outer boundary wall, which enclosed the nuns' quadrangle, is still intact, and in the south-east angle are the remains of a fifteenth-century chapel.

Godstow Nunnery was founded in the reign of King Stephen, and it flourished exceedingly. Fair Rosamund fled here from the wrath of Queen Eleanor. Harried and hunted down, where could she find safer protection than in the Cloister? Actually she died at Woodstock, not many miles away, but her royal lover carried her body to Godstow, and here she was buried in state before the High Altar in the choir of the Nunnery Church, and her tomb, on which was curiously graved in stone the picture of the cup out of which she drank the poison brewed by the Queen, all adorned with flowers, hung with silken tapestries, and lighted with a myriad tapers, became a shrine which drew crowds of worshippers and brought wealth and renown to the community.

Not so many years later there came to Oxford, Bishop Hugh of Lincoln. With his train of clerks and serving-men, he rode out to Godstow upon his caparisoned white mule, as prelates were wont to ride, and the nuns received him reverently at the gate. When he entered the church and saw the tomb, carved with birds, curious fishes and all sort of animals, draped in cloth of gold and shimmering brocades, decked with roses red and white lilies, blazing with lamps and tall wax candles, he turned to the Abbess and asked: "Madam, what manner of sepulchre is this? What Saint rests here?"

"Fair Rosamond" was the reply, "whom King Henry so dearly loved and for whose sweet sake he hath so notably enriched our sisterhood." The grim old bishop sternly knit his brow. "Take her up," he commanded, "and cast her forth into the common cemetery. Be she king's mistress or beggar's drab, she shall not lie in this holy place."

Godstow, they say, is one of the most horribly haunted spots in all England. In the spring and summer the district is a favourite one for campers-out, hikers, and caravaners. It is near a city, and yet right out in the country.

Some seven, or it may be eight years ago, on the afternoon of the last day of April, there came by chance to Godstow a party of three friends, who were driving just as the spirit might move them through Oxfordshire and the Cotswold country. They would drop off for an hour or two here in some little hamlet, see the church, lunch off cheese and cider in the tap-room, and pass on. At night they would put up in one of those quaint old English inns where for a shilling or two you get a little bedroom under the thatch with a sloping roof and tiny latticed windows, with an earthenware ewer and bason, a candle the only light, but spotlessly clean and comfortable, the sheets smelling of lavender, the pillows soft as down. Or else they would camp out in the fields, wrapped in rugs and overcoats, their little canvas tent spread over them. That thirtieth of April had been as hot as mid-July. There was a swim in the river, and dinner at the Trout. Simple English fare, but cooked as only the old-fashioned English cook knows how, the proverbial roast-beef, with its Yorkshire pudding and baked potatoes, the apple tart, the Cheddar cheese. And after dinner coffee on the lawn, and a stroll with a pipe under the starlit sky. Should they sleep at the Trout or in the fields? They all voted for the open air. Was there any objection to camping out on the other bank of the river, in the field near those old ruins? Not the slightest. The place was public. Who did the ruins belong to? The waiter wasn't sure. He thought Oxford University took care of the fabric. Anyway there would be nobody to disturb or threaten them as trespassers, they could count on that.

It was about eleven-o'-clock that Fortescue, Yates, and Brunton spread their rugs under the convent wall and threw themselves wearily down. On the other side of the river, not so far away, the lights in the windows of the Trout were going out one by one. The last glass of ale had been drunk, the bar cleared, the front door closed half-an-hour before. Brunton was already in the land of Nod. Fortescue was snoring, rhythmically. But tired as he was, Yates for some reason lay gazing up at Cassiopeia's Chair and Cepheus overhead, and wondering . . . wondering . . . wondering until he dozed.

What a queer dream! How clear—low yet clear—the sound of the chanting seemed! He could almost distinguish the Latin words sung to some strange melody. And surely that smell—that was incense! Incense in a meadow at midnight—he must be in a church . . . what a mad dream . . . the maddest of dreams! And then he realised he was wide awake.

He sat up with a start. Brunton and Fortescue lay motionless. He could hear their heavy breathing as they slumbered sprawling there. He looked round. Impossible! Light was streaming from the convent windows—streaming through stained glass. He could see the ruby and emerald and gold. But the evening before there had been no windows in that wall, merely empty black gaping holes!

He rubbed his eyes bewildered. Those were voices . . . what was it they were chanting? Gloria in profundis . . . in profundis gloria . . . One thing he felt, danger, some horrible unseen danger was near. Yates, although but a young fellow of two and twenty, was no coward, yet at that moment he says he knew what it meant literally to feel the hair rise on one's head. Anything was better than to lie there. He must find out what was going on. Quietly he rose to his feet, and without a sound crept nearer the ruined wall.

He felt a hand on his arm and only just stifled a cry, he turned, Fortescue was at his side, and Brunton with his finger on his lip. "Shh," he whispered, "we've heard it too!"

Yates nodded dumbly, it was no moment for speech. He dropped on his hands and knees signing to his chums to do the same. In silent file they crawled to the south-east angle of the wall, whence unseen they could see the other side.

Some fifty or sixty persons were assembled. Whether the cowled cloak figures were those of men or women one could not tell. In that open place, the ruins of the ancient chapel, an altar had been set up. Six black candles, whose flame burned without a flicker in the still breathless air, were ranged in equal order to flank a tall crucifix. A caricature of the Cross! It was not that the image lacked the crudest realism, so far as the details of bruises and blood were concerned. These indeed were rendered with a too ghastly fidelity. But the face was one to freeze the very marrow. It was indeed the Christ of Christ's enemies—their hate and mockery had found fullest expression in the bestial blasphemy of that distorted countenance, writhing like a maniac with its awful grin and lolling slobbery tongue!

The silent watchers shuddered and retched at the monstrous insanity, the stark evil of the thing.

Before the altar stood a man vested in a richly laced alb and cope of flaming scarlet embroidered in black with the design of a single large he-goat, squatting on its haunches, bearded and lewd. Two red stones that sparkled and glinted seemed living leering eyes. Lengthwise, along the altar, lay a figure that stirred and moved a little. They could see the gleam of white naked limbs.

On either side of the priest there were stationed two men in ordinary evening dress suits. They were close masked, and wore white gloves. The one held open a large folio from which the celebrant was reading with frenzied mutter and swift secret sign. The other swayed a censer, whence the heady fume filled the air with its pungent acrid smell.

Amid a horrid hush the celebrant suddenly raised above his head a large Host, triangular, with three sharp points, and black.

At this very moment Yates felt his arms pinioned behind him in a strong grasp. As he struggled for a second he saw that Fortescue and Brunton had also been seized and were held prisoners.

He strove to utter a cry . . . his senses reeled.

When Yates opened his eyes he was lying wrapped in his rug where he had lain down to sleep on the grass. It was early. There was the fragrance of a May dawn in the air. The birds were chirping in the trees or busily seeking their first meal on the dewy lawns. He rose to his feet a little unsteadily, conscious a splitting head-ache and a curious sickly smell in his nostrils. Fortescue and Brunton were slumbering a few paces away.

A dip in the cool river and a brisk swim cleared his head, and he was not sorry to see that the Trout began to show signs of life and breakfast. By this time his two friends had joined him in the water.

"Well . . . . was it all a dream . . . just a vivid night-mare?" he asked, as they stood rubbing themselves down with the rough towels.

"No," said Fortescue decisively, "I'll be shot if 'twas a dream. I can feel that devil's grip around my shoulders now. Look where he bruised me."

"By gum, you're right. 'Twas no dream," murmured Brunton meditatively. "Here, let's have a squint at the place."

Half hesitatingly we crossed to the old nunnery wall, and peered round it. A mere empty open space met our gaze.

"I'm jolly well damned . . ."

"No you're not. Look how the grass is crushed and trampled. Oh, there's been a crowd here, sure enough, and not so very long ago either. This is where we stood. See this, sonny," and Fortescue stooped to pick up a little wad of cotton-wool. He sniffed at it warily. "Smell. Not too close! Careful."

"Of course," said Brunton. "I remember now."

"Remember? What?"

"Why, the thirtieth of April. The Eve of May Day. Die Walpurgis-Nacht."

A PARTIAL LIST OF SNUGGLY BOOKS

CPSIA information can be obtained
at www.ICGtesting.com
Printed in the USA
LVHW051703150720
660781LV00007B/1026

9 781645 250395